"I'll call you bac

No sooner had I
than the phone rang

"Boy," she said wi   est
two minutes in history."

There was no answer. She could hear heavy breathing on the other end of the line.

"Jess, cut it out," she warned. "This isn't funny."

"I'll tell you what isn't funny," a deep, muffled, sinister voice replied. "What isn't funny is poking into other people's private business. And hanging around where you're not wanted. Am I making myself clear?"

Elizabeth was so frightened she could barely breathe. "Wh-who is this?" she managed to ask.

"Listen to me, Miss Wakefield," the man snarled. "I know who you are. That's all that matters. Just get this through your pretty blond head. *We're watching you*. We know exactly where you are. And we don't intend to let you get in our way. Do you understand?" He laughed—a dark, awful laugh—and hung up.

Elizabeth was trembling all over. She was completely alone in the office. The lights had been dimmed when people left hours ago. Who was this caller? What if he was calling from inside the building? What if he trapped her here?

Then to her horror, the phone rang again.

After seven rings, she picked it up. "H-hello?" she gasped.

"Liz, where were you?" Jessica demanded. "Didn't I tell you it was only going to be a minute before I called back?"

"Yeah," Elizabeth mumbled, looking around the dark office. She fought hard not to scream. "Jess," she said as calmly as she could. "I'm coming home right away. If I don't get there in fifteen minutes, call the police."

Bantam Books in the Sweet Valley High Series
Ask your bookseller for the books you have missed

SWEET VALLEY HIGH
Super THRILLER

NO PLACE TO HIDE

Written by
Kate William

Created by
FRANCINE PASCAL

BANTAM BOOKS
TORONTO · NEW YORK · LONDON · SYDNEY · AUCKLAND

RL 6, IL age 12 and up

NO PLACE TO HIDE
A Bantam Book / December 1988

Sweet Valley High is a registered trademark of Francine Pascal.

Conceived by Francine Pascal.

*Produced by Daniel Weiss Associates, Inc.,
27 West 20th Street,
New York, NY 10011*

Cover art by James Mathewuse

ISBN 0-553-27554-2

Published simultaneously in the United States and Canada

Bantam Books are published by Bantam Books, a division of Bantam Doubleday
Dell Publishing Group, Inc. Its trademark, consisting of the words "Bantam
Books" and the portrayal of a rooster, is Registered in U.S. Patent and Trademark
Office and in other countries. Marca Registrada. Bantam Books, 666 Fifth Avenue,
New York, New York 10103.

PRINTED IN THE UNITED STATES OF AMERICA

O   0 9 8 7 6 5 4 3 2 1

NO PLACE
TO HIDE

One

"I just can't understand you, Liz," Jessica Wakefield declared, narrowing her blue-green eyes. "How can you get so worked up about a little thing like who wins the race for mayor of Sweet Valley?" She sighed deeply. "Here we are, spending the whole summer working for this newspaper, working even harder than during the school year, and all you can talk about is politics. Don't you ever feel like relaxing in your free time?"

Elizabeth smiled. She was used to hearing her twin object to her ideas. It was something she took as much for granted as their identical appearances. Right now she was trying to get Jessica to see how important the upcoming elec-

1

tion for mayor of Sweet Valley was. Clearly it was going to take some doing!

It was lunchtime on Friday afternoon, and in a few hours the twins would be wrapping up a long week at their summer jobs as interns at *The Sweet Valley News*. Usually July was a quiet month at the paper, but lately it seemed one big story after another had been breaking. A number of reporters were working on Miles Robinson's campaign, and the newspaper had already run an editorial in support of him. In spite of its backing, the other candidate, a businessman named Russell Kincaid, still had the lead in the opinion polls.

"Look how beautiful it is outside," Jessica grumbled, staring out the fifth-floor window. "How'd I get roped into this job, anyway?"

Elizabeth laughed out loud. It had been her idea to sign up for the job at the *News*, and when Jessica hadn't had any specific summer plans, their parents had insisted that she sign up as an intern, too. For Elizabeth, whose lifelong ambition was to be a writer, the job was a dream come true. She and Jessica took turns helping out a few of the young editors on the staff, doing general editorial work, research, and office errands. On Monday they were each going to be given their first full-time assignment to assist a writer doing a major feature! Elizabeth could hardly wait. Her boyfriend, Jeffrey French, was away for the summer working as a camp counselor, so Elizabeth was thrilled to have a job she could throw herself into.

"Sometimes I can't believe we're even related," Jessica complained, still looking out the window. "Aren't twins supposed to have some kind of telepathic ability to feel and like the same things?" She tucked a strand of golden hair behind her ear. "I can't remember the last time you and I liked the same thing. I guess that's probably because it never happened."

Elizabeth giggled. "What about Guido's pizza? We both like that."

But she knew exactly what Jessica meant. It was true. On the outside, Jessica and Elizabeth were mirror images. Silky blond hair, sparkling blue-green eyes, and model-slim figures gave them a quintessential California beauty. They were alike right down to the tiny dimple they each had when they smiled. Although they were both a perfect size six, their styles of dress were very different. Today Elizabeth was wearing a navy blue skirt—slim-cut and flattering, but on the conservative side—and a simple blue-and-white-striped cotton sweater, while Jessica looked as if she had just stepped out of the pages of *Ingenue*, her favorite magazine. She had on a linen miniskirt, a boxy sweater with padded shoulders, and funky dangling earrings.

Elizabeth knew their differences went far below the surface. She tended to be the responsible, hard-working part of the team, while Jessica did whatever she wanted, whenever she felt like doing it!

Now she moaned dramatically, throwing herself back into her chair and rolling it across the floor toward her twin. "I still don't see why you want Miles Robinson to be mayor. I think this guy Kincaid is handsome." Her eyes sparkled. "He looks like one of those guys you see on the cover of a Gothic romance. Dark, rugged, muscular—you know." What Jessica said was true.

Kincaid had enormous charisma. He was in his early sixties and was still a handsome man, with angular, well-pronounced features and rugged good looks. But no one in Sweet Valley knew much about him. He had been a private businessman for years and had made a great deal of money. His business was described as import/export, but it wasn't exactly clear what that entailed.

4

Elizabeth picked up the copy of the *News* lying on her desk to study the picture that had caught her eye. "Russell Kincaid on the Campaign Trail," the headline announced. The brief story beneath explained that Robinson, who had been involved in local politics for years, was facing a serious threat from Mr. Kincaid. "New to politics, Mr. Kincaid claims he is the people's choice for mayor of Sweet Valley."

"I don't know, Jess. There's something about his looks that scares me," Elizabeth objected. She pointed to his eyes, which were fierce and dark. "And you heard what Seth and the other reporters were saying about him. There's been talk about illegal use of campaign funds and bribery."

Jessica tossed back her hair. "I'm surprised at you, Liz. None of that stuff has been proven. And, anyway, I still think he's handsome. Miles Robinson doesn't seem like he'd be a very thrilling mayor."

"Who cares about thrilling, Jess?" Elizabeth asked. "I just think Robinson would make a better mayor than Kincaid. Robinson stands for everything that's important to Sweet Valley. He's hardworking, earnest, and above all, he's honest."

Just then Seth Miller, one of the young reporters, strolled by. "Don't tell me I've walked in on yet another Kincaid versus Robinson debate!"

Jessica pouted and fiddled with a paper clip. "Seth, you don't think Kincaid's a crook like everyone else around here, do you?"

Seth ran his hands through his dark hair. "I wouldn't say he's a crook, Jess, but everything I've read about the guy makes me nervous. I think he's bad news." He frowned. "Unfortunately, he seems to have a charismatic hold on people. Unless we do uncover some real wrongdoing, I don't see how Robinson's going to be able to hold his own when election day rolls around."

"I think you're all nuts," Jessica muttered, still intent on the paper clip. "What kind of evidence is there that he's done anything wrong?"

"Well, that's part of the problem," Seth admitted. "He's allegedly mishandled campaign funds from day one, but no one can prove it. There's also talk of some bad connections he's made in business. He owned a factory in Tijuana that was shut down by the government because of inhumane working conditions. His name has been linked with some people in the world of organized crime as well. But, as I said, it's all just talk so far. People *like* Kincaid. He charms them into thinking he'll be a strong leader." He shrugged. "Unless we can get some solid stuff on him, it looks as though he has a good chance of winning."

Jessica looked triumphantly at her sister. "See, there's nothing wrong with the guy. Liz is completely supporting Robinson," she told Seth, as if she still couldn't believe it.

"Good for you." Seth patted Elizabeth on the shoulder. "My own hunch is that Kincaid is the kind of guy who'll hang himself if we give him enough rope. I think you're rooting for the right guy, Liz. And, incidentally, so does everyone else around here."

Jessica bit her lip. The conversation wasn't going the way she wanted it to, so with characteristic speed she changed the subject.

"Listen, what time is the picnic tomorrow?" she asked. "Have you ever been to this place before, Seth?"

The *News* was holding its annual summer picnic the next day in Ronoma County, a rural area about forty miles southeast of Sweet Valley. Neither of the twins had ever been there, and both had been wondering what it was like.

7

Jessica was afraid there wouldn't be anything to do.

Seth shook his head. "No, I've never been there before. I'm looking forward to finally seeing it. It's supposed to be beautiful. I think people will be arriving around noon. Do you two need a ride?"

"No," Elizabeth said, giving Seth a smile. "But thanks, anyway."

Jessica rolled herself around on her office chair, waiting till Seth had walked away to say, "Why can't they have the picnic someplace nearby, like Secca Lake or the beach? I have a feeling Ronoma is way out in the middle of nowhere!"

Elizabeth shrugged. "It'll be fun to go someplace new, Jess."

Jessica rolled herself back to her own desk. "I don't care whether or not the place is new," she said moodily. "It would be a lot more fun if they'd import a bunch of handsome new reporters and keep it right here in Sweet Valley."

Elizabeth had to laugh. When they had first started their jobs, Jessica had been enchanted by one reporter after another—especially by Seth. But, as usual, she had gotten tired of flirting, especially flirting that led nowhere.

Jessica was chattering on about an article in the latest issue of *Ingenue*, which lay open on her desk. "Liz," she said suddenly, frowning. "Are you listening to a word I'm saying?"

Elizabeth looked up at her twin, dazed. "Sorry," she said, "I was just thinking that I should call Nicholas Morrow back. I got a message that he called." She looked thoughtful as she pulled the telephone closer to her. "Maybe I'll invite him to the picnic. He could use some cheering up."

She didn't know why she hadn't thought of it sooner. Nicholas desperately needed to get out of his house and meet some new people. She was definitely going to ask him to come with them.

"Nicholas?" Elizabeth cleared her throat. "It's Liz Wakefield."

"Oh—hi, Liz," Nicholas said. His voice sounded distant and sad. "Can you hang on for a minute? I'm going to switch phones." She could hear muffled voices, then footsteps as Nicholas moved slowly away. It seemed like ages before he picked up again.

"That's better. Now I'm up in my room, and I can have some privacy." Elizabeth wasn't surprised that Nicholas's voice sounded strained. She knew that he had been depressed lately.

Nicholas Morrow had been a friend ever since his family moved to Sweet Valley. The Morrows were wealthy, and the mansion they had bought up in the hills overlooking the valley rivaled the most luxurious homes in the area. Kurt and Skye Morrow were both strikingly attractive, and their nineteen-year-old son was incredibly handsome, too.

Nicholas had graduated from high school and was working for his father while he made up his mind about what he wanted to study. He had impressed Elizabeth in the time she spent with him as being a bright, fun-loving person, completely devoted to his family. He and Elizabeth had always liked each other as friends. At one time Nicholas had had a crush on her, but she had managed to keep his friendship without turning their relationship into a romance. Nicholas was closer to Elizabeth than to Jessica, but he liked both of them.

Neither of the girls had seen much of Nicholas lately, though. His younger sister, Regina, had died a few months earlier, and sometimes it seemed as if Nicholas would never get over his grief.

Regina, a sweet and beautiful girl, had fallen deeply in love with Bruce Patman, a senior at Sweet Valley High and the son of one of the richest men in town. Everyone had always considered Bruce to be shallow and egotistical, but all that had changed with Regina. He really fell in love with her and for the first time learned to put another person before himself.

When their relationship ended, Regina, despondent and alone, had turned for solace to a boy who was involved with a bad crowd at school—kids who were known for doing drugs. Regina seemed intent on proving that the breakup didn't bother her and one night at a party had decided to try cocaine. She had had an extremely rare reaction to the drug, which caused her heartbeat to accelerate, then brought on sudden cardiac failure.

Everyone at Sweet Valley High was devastated by Regina's death. But Elizabeth was keenly aware that Nicholas was affected more deeply than anyone else. Because he hadn't attended school in Sweet Valley, he had met most of his friends through Regina, and he wasn't particularly close to any of them. He hadn't had a solid group of friends to rely on during this difficult time. His parents had each other, but Nicholas had no one. He had adored his sister, and since her death he had fallen into a deep depression that seemed destined to drag on and on.

Elizabeth was determined to help pull him out of it. A picnic with a new group of people who wouldn't make him think of his sister might be just the thing.

"I got your message, Nicholas. I'm calling you back from the *News* office," Elizabeth told him, glancing at her watch to confirm that she had ten minutes left on her lunch break. "I'm glad you called, because I've been thinking about you. Do you have plans for tomorrow?"

"No," Nicholas said listlessly.

"How are you, anyway?" Elizabeth prompted. "Are you feeling any better these days?"

Nicholas cleared his throat. "Not really, Liz. That's what everyone keeps asking me—my parents, the doctor they've been sending me to see once a week. They keep talking about 'the natural stages of mourning,' and all that stuff. To be honest, though, I've been feeling worse. I called you because my parents keep bugging me about staying in touch with my friends. But it's so hard for me, Liz. All of my friends were Regina's friends, too, and seeing them just reminds me of her."

12

Elizabeth frowned. "Well, it sounds as if you need to get out, Nicholas. I'd love it if you'd come—"

But Nicholas cut her off. "Forget it. There's no point, Liz. Besides being depressed, I'm exhausted all the time. I'm lucky if I sleep four hours a night." He laughed hollowly. "I have the world's most terrible nightmares. I wake up thinking—" His voice broke off. "Never mind," he whispered. "You didn't call back to hear about my dreams."

Elizabeth bit her lip. He sounded even worse than she had imagined. "Nicholas," she said gently, "the newspaper is having a picnic tomorrow about forty miles southeast of Sweet Valley. It's going to be lots of fun. There'll be volleyball games and a big cookout, even fireworks. I want you to come with Jessica and me."

"It's nice of you to think of me, Liz," Nicholas said. "But to be honest with you, I'm not the greatest company these days. Maybe some other time."

"Nicholas," Elizabeth said firmly, "I know this is hard for you, but you can't spend all of your time by yourself." She took a deep breath. "Regina wouldn't have wanted that."

13

Nicholas was silent for a minute. "Maybe you're right," he said finally.

"I really want you to come," Elizabeth said. "It'll be fun, and you'll meet some new people."

Nicholas hesitated. "All right," he said slowly, "I know it will make my parents happy if I go."

He didn't exactly sound excited, but Elizabeth felt victorious when she hung up the phone.

"Guess what?" she said to her sister. "I had to twist his arm, but Nicholas says he'll come with us to the picnic tomorrow."

Jessica stared at her, alarmed. "Haven't you heard what Nicholas has been like lately? Lila says he's losing his mind."

Lila Fowler was one of Jessica's best friends, and she made it her business always to know what was going on in Sweet Valley.

"He isn't losing his mind," Elizabeth responded. "He happens to have been through a terrible trauma, and he could use his friends to cheer him up a little bit."

"Well, Lila heard that he's in such bad shape, his parents are sending him to a psychiatrist." She frowned. "Do you really think it's a good idea to bring him tomorrow?"

"Why not?" Elizabeth asked. "It'll be good for him. Who knows, he might end up having a

14

great time." She turned away from her twin and opened up her notebook, ready to get back to work. As far as she was concerned, the discussion was closed.

Jessica groaned under her breath. How she was going to be able to enjoy herself when Nicholas was with them was more than she could figure out.

She was just going to have to leave Nicholas to Elizabeth. Since it was Elizabeth's idea to bring him along, then Elizabeth could deal with him if he fell apart in the middle of the picnic.

Two

"I told you this wasn't a good idea," Jessica complained. It was Saturday morning, and the twins were waiting for Nicholas to pick them up in his Jeep. The Fiat Spider they shared was a two-seater with a very small, cramped backseat, so they had decided to go to Ronoma in Nicholas's car.

He was already ten minutes late, and Jessica was having a fit. She had spent most of the morning trying to get her hair to stay in some new combs she had bought recently, and now that they were in, she wanted to be on the road.

A car pulled into the drive, and Jessica hurried to the window. "Darn. It's only Steve and Adam," she grumbled. Steven, the twins' older brother, attended a nearby college during the school year. He was sharing his room with his classmate Adam Maitland this summer. Adam was clerking for a law firm in Sweet Valley and couldn't afford to rent a place of his own.

"I thought you two would be long gone by now," Steven said as he and Adam strolled into the foyer. They had been playing tennis, and both looked healthy and ruddy-cheeked from the exercise.

"Yeah," Jessica said, her eyes narrowing, "so did I. But—"

"Look, he's here!" Elizabeth exclaimed with relief as Nicholas turned his Jeep into the drive behind Steven's yellow Volkswagen. "You're incredible," she added to her sister. "Tell me *one* time you can think of when you've been on time! Now, when Nicholas is a mere ten minutes late, you're ready to murder him."

"Aren't you glad you don't have twin sisters?" Steven joked to Adam as the girls pushed their way out the door to meet Nicholas.

It had been awhile since Elizabeth had last seen him, and she was struck by the change in his appearance. He had lost a lot of weight, his skin was pale, and he had dark shadows under his eyes. Elizabeth could hardly believe this was the same handsome boy she had become friends with.

She gave him an impulsive hug. "How're you doing?" she asked as Jessica clambered into the back of the Jeep.

Nicholas frowned. "I'm all right." He brushed his hair back and slipped on a pair of dark sunglasses. "Sorry I'm late. It took me forever to get going this morning."

Elizabeth looked at him with concern. "Didn't you sleep well?"

Nicholas got back into the Jeep and started it up as she jumped into the passenger seat. He shrugged, then glanced briefly in the rearview mirror. "Nah, not so great. I have these nightmares sometimes about Regina. Well, they're not exactly nightmares. I just hear . . ." He shuddered. "I don't know, it's like I can hear her voice or something."

"Ugh!" Jessica exclaimed from the backseat.

Elizabeth shot her a look. Jessica sure knew how to sound sympathetic. "Oh, Nicholas. That must be frightening. I think this picnic is going to be perfect for you. Getting away from Sweet Valley, meeting new people . . ."

"Well," Jessica said dubiously, "I'm not sure how fascinating any of the people who work for the newspaper are going to seem to Nicholas."

Nicholas sighed. He was gripping the wheel tightly. "I really appreciate both of you making the effort. But. . . ." His voice trailed off, and he didn't say anything for a minute. An uncomfortable silence followed, and Elizabeth could hear Jessica clearing her throat. She knew exactly what her twin was thinking.

Why had they brought Nicholas along?

The *News* picnic was being held in a lovely park in Ronoma County. A crystal-blue pond was surrounded by rolling green landscape. When the twins and Nicholas arrived a number of people were sitting at the picnic tables near the barbecue. Cheerful music was blaring from someone's portable tape player.

"Hi, guys!" Darcy Kaymen called as they approached. "Come on over and help me demolish this fried chicken!" Darcy was also working for the *News* as an intern for the summer. Red-haired and loud, Elizabeth found Darcy somewhat abrasive. But Darcy and Jessica had become friends.

Nicholas hung back, and Elizabeth had to take his arm to urge him to meet people. Most of the younger reporters were there, and many of the editors had brought their families along. Elizabeth noticed Dan Weeks and Seth Miller trying to organize a volleyball game. It was a beautiful summer day, and she felt the festive spirit starting to infect her.

"Come meet Seth," she said to Nicholas.

But Nicholas seemed reluctant to participate in the merriment. He went along with introductions in a slightly stiff, reserved manner, as if he were just waiting for each conversation to end so he could be alone again. He kept looking around nervously. "What's the name of this park?" he asked Seth, interrupting a comment the reporter had been making about Robinson's mayoral race.

Seth was surprised. "Let me see . . . I think it's just called Ronoma Point Park. This area was a very popular beach community about fifty years ago. There are still a number of big old houses left over from those days, and in fact, I've heard people in Sweet Valley saying this area may be rediscovered soon. People are buying some of the old places, starting to fix them up."

Elizabeth glanced at Nicholas. She wished she could think of some way to get him to loosen up a bit. "Nicholas, I'm ready for some of that chicken. How about you?"

Nicholas shook his head. "No, I'm not hungry, Liz." He avoided her worried gaze. "In fact, to be honest, what I really feel like doing is taking a walk." He glanced up at the woods behind the pond. "I think it would do me a lot of good to get some exercise, kind of clear my head. Do you mind?"

The last thing Nicholas needed was to take a solitary walk through the woods, Elizabeth thought. Hadn't the whole point been to introduce him to people, to try to draw him out of his depression?

But Nicholas was her guest. If he wanted to take a walk, she felt she should go with him. "Seth," Elizabeth said in a low voice, "I think I'm going to take a walk with Nicholas. If anyone wonders where I am . . ."

"Go ahead! Enjoy yourself," Seth boomed, moving back in the direction of the food. Elizabeth felt her heart sink. She didn't think it was right to wander off from a company gathering this way. But she wasn't going to let Nicholas go off by himself, either.

"Hey!" Elizabeth gasped, hurrying after him as he started up the gravelly path that led around the lake to the woods behind it. "Wait for me!"

Nicholas frowned. "You stay, Liz. I know you're having fun talking to people. I really don't mind being by myself for a little while."

"What if I happen to want to take a walk, too?" Elizabeth demanded, falling into step beside him.

Nicholas didn't say anything for a moment.

But when he looked at her, he said, very gently, "Thanks."

And Elizabeth knew then that she had done the right thing by coming with him. They walked almost the whole way around the pond. Nicholas kept his hands jammed in his pockets, his eyes on the path. Elizabeth glanced appreciatively around her. The lush park was filled with flowers and birds, and the sunlight sparkled on the water. Elizabeth could feel Nicholas relaxing a little bit as they walked.

Neither of them spoke. It seemed much better just to walk together in silence, enjoying the natural beauty surrounding them.

Nicholas stopped at the far end of the pond, shaded his eyes with his hands, and looked with interest at an unpaved road running off through the woods. They could still hear the animated sounds of the picnic from across the pond. "Liz," he said, "you can go back if you like. I want to walk up and see what's through the woods."

Elizabeth looked back across the pond. She knew if they started exploring they wouldn't be back for ages. But much as she wanted to go back, she wasn't going to leave Nicholas. "I'm game," she said with as much enthusiasm as she could muster.

About a quarter of a mile farther on, the unpaved road met the main road that they had driven on earlier. But the unpaved road intersected it, continuing up a hill, and Nicholas followed it, with Elizabeth right behind him. They could see houses in the distance up on the cliffs overlooking the ocean. Nicholas wanted to go up and take a closer look at them and get a view of the sea.

The houses proved to be farther apart from each other than they appeared, and Nicholas and Elizabeth found themselves approaching a wrought-iron gate closing off an expanse of land leading to a large gray clapboard house. A wooden board hanging on the gate was painted in bold black letters. It read "Bayview House." Nicholas tested the gate. It was unlocked, and he pushed it open and strolled up the driveway. Elizabeth hung back, and Nicholas had to turn to urge her to follow. "I don't know," Elizabeth said uneasily. "Isn't it—I mean, should we really . . ."

But Nicholas had already gone ahead. She had no choice but to follow.

Something seemed peculiar about the house and grounds. The grass was wild and uncut, and the paint on the house was peeling. Everything suggested a state of general disrepair, but

Elizabeth didn't have the feeling that the place was deserted. As they walked closer, she noticed a car parked along the right side of the house. "Nicholas, someone lives here. There's a car over there."

"I guess you're right," Nicholas said. "Maybe we shouldn't be trespassing here." The sound of his voice was very loud in the stillness. He laughed awkwardly but continued walking. "Come on, Liz," he called to her. "Let's go take a look at the cliffs and the ocean."

They were halfway across the untended yard when Elizabeth saw something that made her stop short. In the middle of the unkempt grass, a perfectly manicured garden had been set off by a small fence. Rosebushes were neatly tied back, all sorts of flowers grew in luxurious rows, and the whole garden looked as though it had been watered that very morning.

Elizabeth froze. "What's that?" she demanded. She thought she could hear someone singing. It seemed to be coming from the woods to their left, a low, haunting melody that she didn't recognize. Nicholas glanced around.

"I don't know. I hear it, too," he whispered. "You think we should get out of here?"

Before Elizabeth could answer, she heard the unmistakable yap of a little dog. Then came another, followed by a whole explosion of little barks. A tiny Yorkshire terrier came tearing out of the woods and ran in circles around Nicholas. Still barking, it jumped at Nicholas's legs, then leaped up at Elizabeth.

"Rory! Rory!" a clear voice called. Nicholas and Elizabeth stood frozen. They were trespassing on somebody's property, and now they were going to be caught! Nicholas tried to pat the little dog, but its incessant barking just got louder.

"Rory, *stop* that," the voice commanded. And as Nicholas glanced up, a young girl came hurrying out of the woods, her arms full of wildflowers. She stopped short when she saw Nicholas. "Oh—" she said, her eyes growing wide. She glanced past him to Elizabeth, a look of curiosity and pleasure on her face.

Elizabeth noticed Nicholas was staring at the girl. She wasn't surprised. She had never seen anyone as beautiful in her whole life. The girl looked about sixteen or seventeen. Her face was perfectly oval, and her skin, a creamy color, was protected from the sun by a straw bonnet. Her hair fell down almost to her waist; it was a rich chestnut brown that gleamed in the sunlight. And her eyes . . . Elizabeth had never seen eyes like hers before—huge, wide-set, light

26

blue eyes, fixed on Nicholas with a look of curiosity and surprise. Even though she had obviously been running in the woods with her dog, she was wearing a dress, a lovely sky-blue silk dress, longer than most girls wore, with a slightly old-fashioned bodice.

The girl gazed briefly at Elizabeth but couldn't seem to take her eyes from Nicholas's face once she looked back at him.

"Hello," she said. The flowers went slack in her arms, and she tilted her head to one side, staring at him.

"Uh, hello," Nicholas stammered. "I—I know we shouldn't be walking around here. I mean, we should have rung the bell or knocked or—we were just—we wanted to look at the view," he explained.

The girl gave him a radiant smile that seemed to light up her face. "I'm glad," she said simply. She looked down at the dog, which had stopped its yapping the minute she approached. "Shame on you, Rory. That's no way to treat company," she chided him.

Nicholas took a deep breath. He looked as if he felt he'd stumbled into some kind of beautiful dream and he was afraid anything he said would make the girl disappear. "I should introduce myself," he managed to say. "My name is

Nicholas. Nicholas Morrow. I live in Sweet Valley. Have you ever heard of it?"

The girl shook her head, her long hair swinging.

"No," she said. "But I'm a complete stranger here. I just came to California a few weeks ago. I grew up—well, it's a long story. I don't know the area at all." She turned to Elizabeth. "My name is Barbara. What's yours?"

"Elizabeth."

"Well, Elizabeth and Nicholas," Barbara said, "I'd ask you to have a cup of tea inside, but Josine, that's our housekeeper, hasn't been feeling well today, and I don't think—" She shook her head. "She's very old," she whispered. "I think sometimes she doesn't remember things very clearly. She gets me mixed up with my grandmother, who she took care of when she was a girl my age."

Nicholas looked up at the big house. "Do you have a large family? It looks like there's a lot of room in that house."

Barbara shook her head. "No, there's only me. But, anyway, this isn't my house." She glanced from Elizabeth to Nicholas. "I grew up in Switzerland," she went on. "This is the house where my grandmother grew up. So when my Uncle John invited me to come for the summer, I decided to take him up on it and learn more

28

about the place where she had lived," she continued. "He's been writing my parents for months, making all the arrangements. He even came over and met them. And it's all worked out just the way we planned it." She stooped to pat Rory. "I brought Rory with me from home," she added. "My parents are both professors, and they're doing research on a Greek island this summer. So it worked out well for me to come here. I've always wanted to see California."

Nicholas listened with fascination. "Who lives here with you, then? Your uncle and the housekeeper? Or your grandmother?"

Barbara shook her head. "My grandmother died when she was very young. That's one of the reasons I was curious to come. None of us knew very much about her. She drowned when my mother was just a baby. My uncle's staying here while I'm visiting, but he usually lives someplace else. And Josine lives here year-round. I don't know why the house was never sold—it must have had something to do with my great-grandfather's will." She paused and looked out at the cliffs behind the house.

Then she turned back to Elizabeth and Nicholas. "So I can't offer you tea," she said again. "But we could sit together for a while."

Nicholas nodded enthusiastically. "Or you

could show us the view from the cliffs," he said eagerly.

Barbara frowned. A faint shadow crossed her face, and she bent down to pet Rory. "Let's stay here," she murmured. "It's silly, I know, but I don't like the cliffs. I think it comes from Josine," she said simply. "She hates for me to go near them. She's frightened of them, so now I am, too. Sometimes my uncle makes me walk Rory there, though. He says I need to get over my fear." She shuddered.

Nicholas put his hand on her arm protectively. "Let's just sit here in the garden, then, and talk," he said.

Barbara seemed pleased. She led them to a cluster of white iron chairs in the garden, and they all sat down, while Rory continued to run around them in circles.

"Tell me about Sweet Valley. Is that where you're both from?" she asked shyly.

Nicholas did most of the talking, and Elizabeth sat back and listened with enjoyment. It was great to see him talking animatedly at last, almost like the old Nicholas. The walk seemed to have done wonders for him. He told Barbara about all the places his family had ever lived, about their home in Sweet Valley, about his father's company. He practically told her his life story. The only topic he didn't bring up was Regina, and Elizabeth got the sense that he didn't want to spoil the afternoon by telling Barbara about his sister's death.

Barbara listened attentively. She asked questions from time to time but mostly just sat quietly, her gaze fastened on Nicholas's face.

"Maybe I could show you Sweet Valley," Nicholas suggested. "It's very pretty. Different from this place, but pretty, too."

"Yes," Barbara said faintly. "I'd like that." She seemed to be straining to hear something, and finally she turned back in the direction of the house. "Did you hear someone calling me?" she asked anxiously.

Nicholas shook his head.

But just then Elizabeth heard a feeble voice calling.

"That's Josine," Barbara said, jumping to her feet and scooping Rory up in her arms. "I have to go."

She turned and hurried across the lawn toward the house.

"Wait!" Nicholas cried, chasing after her.

Barbara only turned back once. "I'm sorry," she said softly, her eyes luminous and wide. "I have to go in." She looked extremely upset. "It isn't Josine I'm worried about. It's Uncle John.

If I don't come as soon as I'm called, he gets incredibly angry."

Nicholas looked distraught. "But he's your uncle," he said slowly. "Why would he get angry with you?"

A look of pain crossed Barbara's lovely face. "No, he really isn't. He's my grandfather's cousin—and he's the executor of my grandmother's will. He takes care of the place, and he's terribly strict." She glanced back with alarm. Just then Elizabeth and Nicholas saw a large, dark-haired man opening the front door and staring in their direction, his expression menacing. Barbara saw him, too. "I have to go," she said hastily. "I'm so happy to have met you both!" With that, she turned and ran to the house, where the man was waiting.

Nicholas didn't move an inch until Barbara disappeared through the front door. Then he turned slowly and faced Elizabeth. "I can't believe I didn't get her last name or her phone number," he said, sounding frustrated. "How am I ever going to get in touch with her?"

Three

On the drive back from the picnic, Elizabeth and Nicholas began to tell Jessica about Bayview House and Barbara.

"I knew I should've come with you. Sounds like you guys had all the fun," Jessica complained. "All anyone at the picnic talked about was the race between Kincaid and Robinson. It was really boring."

Elizabeth glanced at Nicholas. She wasn't sure how much Nicholas wanted to say about Barbara. She had a feeling that he had fallen instantly in love with the beautiful young girl and would want to keep some of the details of their visit to himself.

But she was wrong. Nicholas wanted to talk.

"Liz, tell Jess how strange she started to act

when that housekeeper, Josine, called her back inside." But before Elizabeth could oblige, he started to tell Jessica himself. "She got so scared all of a sudden. I mean, at first she was just perfectly natural. Very open and friendly and everything. Then, the instant this old woman called her name, she panicked completely. And then this man—he's a distant cousin of hers, but she calls him uncle—came to the door and glared at us." He tightened his grip on the steering wheel. "I'd like to know what kind of hold they have over her," he muttered.

"Maybe she was just brought up differently than we were," Elizabeth suggested. "She did say she was raised in Switzerland. Maybe her parents are very strict."

"They can't be too strict," Nicholas objected. "They let her come to California all by herself this summer."

"Will one of you please explain to me *who* this girl is and why you're so intrigued by her?" Jessica exclaimed impatiently.

Elizabeth laughed. "You explain, Nicholas."

"She's . . ." Nicholas's voice faltered. "Well, we took this walk, like we told you. We found this old house up on the cliffs, and we were sort of wandering around when we heard someone singing. Then a little terrier came racing

out, and Barbara was right behind him. Barbara
. . . the most beautiful girl I've ever seen," Nicholas said in a dreamy voice.

Elizabeth gave Jessica a knowing look and smiled. Nicholas was certainly in a much better mood than he had been in during the drive out to the picnic.

"Her grandmother was raised in Bayview House," Nicholas went on. "And Barbara came to spend the summer here because this guy—this cousin or uncle or whatever—invited her."

"When are you going to see her again?" Jessica asked.

Nicholas shrugged. "Well, that's the problem. She ran off so quickly when Josine called her, I didn't have time to get her phone number. Or even find out her last name," he added. "Can you believe it?"

"So, what difference does that make?" Jessica said. "You know where she lives. All you have to do is drive back tomorrow and find her. How hard can it be?"

Elizabeth nodded. "Jessica's right, Nicholas. You should go back right away."

"You really think so?" he asked.

"Absolutely," the twins said in unison.

Elizabeth looked out the window and smiled. She couldn't help feeling that the trip to Ronoma

35

had been a success. Maybe she hadn't gotten much of a chance to talk to the other newspaper people, but at least Nicholas had made a new friend. And something told her they would all be seeing and hearing a lot more about the mysterious and beautiful Barbara from Bayview House.

"See?" Elizabeth said to Jessica, once Nicholas had dropped them off at home. "I told you it was a good idea to bring him along."

Jessica nodded. "Well, I have to hand it to you. Not only did you escape lots of boring political talk by going for a walk, but it looks like you may have found just the thing to help Nicholas get over his depression!"

Elizabeth looked thoughtfully at her sister. "Jess, it was the strangest thing, watching Barbara. I don't know how to describe it, but she really looked frightened when Josine called her. I wonder why."

Jessica shrugged. "There probably isn't any deep explanation, Liz. If she's a stranger here, and doesn't know these people, she may just be worried about how to behave."

"I'm not so sure," Elizabeth said. "I got such a strong sense of her as a person. And she

36

doesn't seem like someone who would scare easily, without reason."

"You just want something to worry about," Jessica teased her. "Now that you don't have Nicholas to worry about, you've decided to worry about Barbara instead. Anyway, Nicholas is going to go back there soon. He'll find out if anything weird is going on."

But Elizabeth wasn't convinced. She pictured the look of fear on Barbara's beautiful face. Something—or someone—was definitely frightening her at Bayview House.

Nicholas barely slept that night. All he could think about was driving back to Ronoma and Bayview House and seeing Barbara again.

On Sunday morning he was even too excited to eat. He left the house early and drove the forty miles to Ronoma in a state somewhere between anticipation and anxiety. What would it be like, seeing her again, this time alone? Would he even find her? Would she be glad to see him?

It was another beautiful, sparkling day, and he was in high spirits when he parked his Jeep on the shoulder of the road near the long drive-way. He hopped out and quickly approached the heavy wrought-iron gate. When it didn't open right away, Nicholas felt his heart fill with fear. Was it locked? But it was just the rusted catch that kept it from opening. He pushed harder, and it gave way.

Nicholas studied the house closely as he crossed the untended lawn. It was a style of architecture that he knew had been very popular, especially along the coast, earlier in the century and forties—a great big wooden house with lots of turrets and a widow's walk affording a view of the sea. At one time Nicholas was sure it must have been gorgeous. Now, though its grandeur remained, it looked more than a little neglected. He wondered why Barbara's uncle didn't take better care of the house.

Nicholas took a deep breath and started up the brick path to the front door. What had once been a clear walkway was now completely overgrown by weeds. Maybe he could help Barbara clear it, he thought. He wiped his hands on his jeans, embarrassed to discover they were sweaty. He was very nervous about seeing her again.

The front door of Bayview House had no door bell, only a large brass knocker. Nicholas lifted it, let it fall, and then repeated the whole procedure for good luck. It was only ten-thirty in the morning—he hoped he hadn't come too early. Both nervous and excited, he shifted his weight from one foot to the other. What was taking so long?

After what seemed like forever, the front door opened. A heavy-set, dark-haired man who appeared to be in his fifties opened the door. He had the kind of face that could have been handsome if its expression wasn't so unpleasant. He was definitely the same man they had seen the day before. Nicholas guessed he was Uncle John. "What do you want?" the man demanded in a gruff, distinctly unfriendly voice.

"Uh—hello." No wonder Barbara was afraid of him. He looked anything but welcoming. "I—uh, I've come to see Barbara. That is, if she's up yet."

The man looked at him with a mixture of fury and disbelief. "How do you know Barbara?" he demanded. Before Nicholas could respond, the man added, "She isn't here. And even if she were, she is not allowed to see young men." His eyes flashing with anger, he started to close the door.

Nicholas couldn't believe his ears. "Please," he began again. "I need to ask her—"

The man's expression darkened. "You heard me," he hissed. "Now get out of here. And if you know what's good for you, you won't ever set foot on this property again." With that, he pulled the heavy door closed.

Nicholas was stunned. "But wait—" he started to shout.

It was too late. The door was closed.

The thought of this tyrant being allowed to bully Barbara made Nicholas furious. No wonder she was so frightened of him!

He slumped down on the porch. None of this made the slightest bit of sense. Why wouldn't this man let Barbara see people? Was he keeping her prisoner here? Nicholas couldn't bear the thought of not ever seeing her again. He had to get a message to her somehow.

Nicholas stared disconsolately at the upstairs windows of Bayview House. What could he do? He could hardly start scaling the walls. If he tried to break in, who knew what her uncle would try to do to him?

No, he was just going to have to face the fact that he couldn't see Barbara. Completely dejected, he walked slowly back down the walk and through the weedy grounds to the iron gate.

Maybe I just dreamed it all, he thought. *Maybe Barbara was just a beautiful vision. I'll get back to Sweet Valley, and Liz will tell me I made the whole thing up.* He was practically crying by the time he got back into his Jeep and started up the engine. He wanted to see Barbara more than anything in the world. What was he going to do?

For the next half mile or so he drove slowly. The top of the Jeep was off, and he could hear birds twittering in the branches as he drove past Ronoma Park. Then he heard something else, faintly at first, then a bit louder. It was a dog barking.

Nicholas pulled the Jeep over, turned it off, and jumped out. Nothing but silence—silence and the birds. And then he heard it again, a distinctive high yap. "Rory!" he cried, tearing through the thick brush in the direction of the sound. "Barbara!"

He stopped running, his heart now beating hard. He no longer heard the barking. *This is nuts*, he told himself. *I must be losing it*. He wiped his forehead, which was damp, and he looked around for a trail to follow into the woods. That was when he heard an unmistakable voice singing the same haunting melody he'd heard the day before. This time he could make out the words:

"You came to me
from out of nowhere.

41

You took my heart
and found it free . . ."

Nicholas felt a shiver run up his spine. Then he heard the bark again.

After taking a deep breath, he forged ahead until he came to a small clearing in the woods. Then he stopped short. The scene before him was like something out of a beautiful impressionistic painting. Rory, tethered to a small tree, was bouncing around on his leash, barking exuberantly. And not far away from him, Barbara, looking resplendent in a pink-and-ivory silk dress, was sitting on an ivory-colored blanket, her legs tucked under her, her long hair gleaming in the sunlight. Her straw bonnet was thrown carelessly next to her on the blanket, and a novel was open on her lap.

"Barbara!" he cried, his whole face lighting up.

In her surprise she knocked the novel off her lap. Looking up at him in delight, she exclaimed, "Nicholas! How on earth did you find me here?" She couldn't seem to believe her eyes. "I'm so glad you came! But I thought . . ." She blushed. "I didn't think you'd ever be able to find me. And Uncle John . . ."

Nicholas stared at her. "I—uh, I went up to

the house. To Bayview House. I knocked and asked for you, but—"

A shadow crossed her face. "So you talked to him," she said, miserable. "He didn't say anything mean to you, did he?"

Nicholas felt an instinctive desire to protect her. "No," he said gently. "But he did make it pretty clear he didn't want me to come back!"

Barbara looked uncomfortable, and she didn't meet his gaze. "He's very strict," she murmured. "He promised my parents he wouldn't let me date. I guess—we probably won't be able to meet if he knows about it."

"You can't tell me not to come back," Nicholas cried. "I won't be able to stand it!"

Barbara looked at him pleadingly. "Nicholas, you must *never* knock on the door again. We'll have to meet somewhere else, not at the house. I can't tell you more about it now, but Uncle John . . . well, just take my word for it. Promise me that you won't ever let him know you're here."

Nicholas swallowed hard. The thought of being able to see her again was so much more important than how or where they met that he would have promised her anything. But he still couldn't understand her uncle's logic.

"Can't you explain to him that it's natural for

you to want to see people your own age? To make friends?"

Barbara shook her head. "It's really complicated, Nicholas. I wish I could explain it all to you, but . . . well, I can't. It just isn't a good idea for him to know if you come to see me here. OK? We can meet," she added, "but it'll have to be our secret." She tried to sound playful, but Nicholas could detect the strain in her voice.

He nodded. "Tell me which room in the house is yours. When I come, I can throw pebbles up to the window to let you know I'm here, like they do on TV."

"It's the second window upstairs, in the back," she told him. "But you'll have to be very careful, Nicholas." She blushed then and looked down at her hands. "If you come back . . ." she said in a whisper.

"What do you mean, if?" Nicholas demanded.

"When I saw you yesterday," she said softly, "it was exactly like something out of a dream. I couldn't believe Rory had found you." She blushed again. "That girl you were with. She's so pretty. Is she your girlfriend?"

"Elizabeth?" Nicholas laughed and shook his head. "No, she's just a good friend. Her boyfriend is away working as a camp counselor for the summer."

Barbara blushed more deeply. "That was such a dumb question," she said, still not meeting his eyes. "It's just that, lately, I haven't been talking to people my own age. The past few weeks have been so strange, living here alone with Josine and Uncle John. I just feel overwhelmed, I guess." Barbara shrugged, and a faint smile crossed her face. Nicholas couldn't get over how beautiful she was.

"So can I come back and see you? Soon?" Nicholas asked eagerly.

Her eyes lit up. "Please," she said. "If I know you're coming, everything will be so much easier."

He almost reached out to touch her then, but he resisted. "You can count on it," he said, his eyes fixed tenderly on hers. "I'll come to see you as often as you like."

"Just as long as you remember what I said before. You can't let my uncle know you're here," she told him. She looked at her watch and sighed. "I have to leave. I promised Josine. . . ." She stood up. "But if I know you're coming back, things won't seem so terrible."

Nicholas jumped to his feet, too. "At least give me your phone number so I can call you," he pleaded.

Barbara shook her head. "I can't. He wouldn't like that at all. Don't call, Nicholas. Don't try."

Nicholas gazed at her beautiful face, feeling utterly confused. Why was her uncle so strict with her? It didn't make any sense. Barbara had told him very little about the man, but he could see how uneasy it made her to talk about him.

"Will you come tomorrow?" she asked, hastily gathering up the blanket and untying Rory.

"I have to work during the day," Nicholas said. "But I'll come back tomorrow evening about seven-thirty, if that's OK with you."

"That would be wonderful," Barbara said, and smiled. "From the road, you'll see a little trail. Follow it through the woods. It winds around to the back of the house. Throw a stone at my window, and I'll come down. I'll meet you in the woods."

Nicholas nodded. He knew he would be living for their next meeting. He could barely stand to watch her run off, with Rory yapping beside her. As he turned to go back to his car, he felt overwhelmed with curiosity. He had to find out more about her. He wanted to know *everything*. It wasn't going to be easy—not with her uncle watching her every minute. But he wasn't going to give up!

Four

Monday morning the twins were at the *News* office early, eager to get their new assignments from Lawrence Robb, features editor of the paper.

"I'm really hoping Mr. Robb gives me something good," Jessica said excitedly. "Lila told me that the mall is doing a special make-over workshop this coming weekend. Maybe Mr. Robb will let me cover it. I could be the new glamour and beauty writer—and I could get a free make-over at the same time."

"If the make-over workshop at the mall is the biggest story Mr. Robb can give you, we're all in trouble," Elizabeth teased her. She was excited about the prospect of the assignment as well. So far the twins had helped research parts of stories, but this would be their first assignment to assist a feature from beginning to end. It was a sign that Mr. Robb liked their work so far and was willing to trust them with a more serious task.

Mr. Robb, an attractive, middle-aged man who had been at the *News* for almost twenty years, was always at his desk by eight o'clock. Even so, he looked surprised when the twins knocked on his door at eight forty-five.

"My," he said, taking off his glasses and looking at them with a smile. "What brings you two carbon copies in at this hour? Don't tell me you're starting to catch the newsroom bug!"

"We were wondering about our assignments, sir," Jessica said forthrightly.

Mr. Robb laughed at the earnest expression on her face. "Oh, yes. I'd forgotten that today was the day." He opened the big file he kept at one side of his desk and thumbed through papers, muttering to himself, "Let's see." When he looked up again, he regarded Jessica. "It still beats me how people tell you two apart," he murmured, "but I'm going to use years of investigative reporting skills and guess that you're Jessica. Am I right?"

"Right!" Jessica exclaimed. "How did you know?"

Mr. Robb pointed at her wrist. "No watch. Your sister never takes hers off."

The twins looked at each other and giggled. Mr. Robb was right. Jessica had often been teased by her family for operating on what they referred to affectionately as Jessica Standard Time. But the girls were surprised Mr. Robb had been paying such close attention.

"OK, Jessica," Mr. Robb said, giving her a smile. "I've assigned you to work with Dan Weeks on covering a new exhibition opening at the Sweet Valley Art Museum. They're going to be displaying a series of paintings by an artist named Paul Lazarow, who headed an artists' colony in Ronoma County in the forties. We don't know very much about the artist, who's dead now, and we want to run a big feature story to coincide with the exhibition. I've already assigned Dan to the story, and I've told him you'll be his assistant. How does that sound to you?"

Jessica's eyes sparkled. "It sounds great," she said. Paintings might not be as instantaneously appealing as a make-over workshop at the mall, but Jessica thought the story sounded romantic and intriguing.

"Now, for you, Liz," Mr. Robb added, riffling through the file. "I was thinking . . ." He cleared his throat and looked directly at her. "I've asked Seth to work on a special feature we're compiling on the mayoral candidates. We want to run two major pieces, one on each of the men involved. It's a very big assignment, and Seth is going to need a lot of help. Do you think you'd be able to take this on?"

Elizabeth nodded, her eyes wide. "I'd love to," she said promptly. "I've been really interested in the election, and I'd love to learn more about Robinson and Kincaid."

"Good," Mr. Robb said with a smile. "Well, that's that, then. Both of you should be in touch with the reporters you're assisting as soon as possible. And good luck!"

"I can't believe you got stuck with that election again," Jessica commiserated as they made their way back to their desks.

Elizabeth stared at her. "What do you mean? This is the best story I could have been given! Do you realize this means I get to spend the next few weeks finding out everything I can about Russell Kincaid?"

Jessica groaned. "Yuck," she pronounced. "I just feel bad 'cause my story's so much more *interesting* than yours."

Elizabeth shook her head. "I don't see why it has to be a competition. But if you put it that

50

way, I'd rather be researching politics than paintings." She narrowed her eyes. "Imagine how great it would be to find out what Russell Kincaid is really like—how he came up with all that money, whether or not he's really dishonest."

Jessica looked at her twin with despair. "Poor Liz," she said sadly. "Well, when you get sick of Russell Kincaid, you can always help me out on the Lazarow exhibition."

Elizabeth smiled but didn't respond. There was no point in trying to explain it to Jessica, but the prospect of researching the two politicians thrilled her.

Who knew what she might uncover?

"Hey," Jessica protested as Elizabeth turned the Fiat into the driveway leading to the Morrow mansion. "Where are we going? I told you, I'm supposed to meet Lila soon." It was Monday evening, and the twins were on their way home from work.

"I want to stop by the Morrows' to see how Nicholas is doing," Elizabeth told her sister. "Come on," she added. "It'll only take a minute. Aren't you curious to hear about his visit with Barbara yesterday?"

Jessica reconsidered. "I guess so," she said.

Elizabeth parked the car and turned off the ignition.

"Hey!" Nicholas called as soon as the twins jumped out of the Fiat. He was standing in the driveway beside his Jeep, and it looked as if he were on his way out. He had on tan chinos, and his hair was still wet from a recent shower. He looked happier and healthier than he had in ages.

"What brings you two here?" he asked, grinning broadly.

"We wanted to hear about your trip to Ronoma yesterday," Elizabeth explained, "and to see if you'd learned any more about the mysterious Barbara from Bayview House." She grinned at him. "Something tells me we may not have come at a good time. You definitely look like a guy who's about to go out on a date."

Nicholas laughed. "To tell you the truth, I *was* about to drive back out there. I told Barbara I'd come out to see her tonight."

"Wow," Jessica said, letting out a low whistle. "Three days in a row. This is starting to sound serious, Nicholas."

Nicholas blushed slightly and shook his head. "Well, we haven't spent a whole lot of time together yet. They've been pretty short visits. But, anyway, how would you two like to come

52

out there with me tonight? I've got some stuff I want to tell you about, and to be honest, I'd really like to know your opinion about the uncle of Barbara's who's taking care of her while she's here."

"You want us to crash your date?" Jessica asked, puzzled.

"Well, it isn't exactly a date." Nicholas sighed. "You see, Barbara made it clear to me that she didn't want me coming around Bayview House at times when anyone could see me or find out I was there. It's all got to be secret." He frowned. "Take tonight, for instance. I'm supposed to give her a secret signal to let her know I'm there. Then she'll come out and meet me. Do you guys want to come?"

Elizabeth glanced at Jessica. "We'd have to call Mom and Dad. Did you say you had plans with Lila?"

"Oh, nothing that can't wait," Jessica said, her eyes sparkling. "I want to see Bayview House and meet Barbara. Not to mention this terrible Uncle John!"

Elizabeth shivered. "I'm all for coming with you, but running into Barbara's uncle is something I definitely don't want to do. You should see him, Jess. He's totally creepy."

While Jessica went into the Morrows' house

to call Lila and cancel their plans and let her parents know they'd be home late, Elizabeth asked Nicholas a few more questions about Barbara.

"Did you get more of a sense of what she's like?"

Nicholas nodded. "Yeah, I did. Liz, I really like her. In fact, I don't think I've ever met anyone who's made me feel this way before. She's bright and gentle, and there's a real solidness to her personality." He shook his head. "Do you think it's possible to fall in love with someone in just a couple of days? That's what it feels like is happening. She's all I can think about."

"Nicholas, that's wonderful!" Elizabeth cried. She could hardly believe this was the same boy she had been so worried about over the weekend. He really seemed like a new person.

"It is," Nicholas agreed. "But at the same time it's making me uneasy that she seems so restricted there. The impression I've gotten is that her uncle isn't treating her well. It's strange. I mean, he could just be really strict, but I get the feeling it's more than that. She hasn't told me anything much, but I can tell that she's frightened of him."

"I noticed that, too," Elizabeth murmured. "I wonder why."

Nicholas shook his head. "I know she's worried about my interfering, too," he added. "She seems to feel it could be dangerous for me if her uncle found out I was there. But that doesn't make sense to me either."

"It's OK with Mom and Dad," Jessica announced as she came back outside.

"Let's go," Nicholas said, opening the passenger side of the Jeep. "Leave the Fiat here, and we'll stop back for it later."

On the way out to Ronoma, Nicholas filled Jessica in on what he had told Elizabeth.

"I think everyone's overreacting," Jessica said. "After all, Barbara grew up in Europe. She doesn't know these people or this place at all. Maybe she's just being paranoid about simple overprotective behavior."

"I doubt it, Jess," Elizabeth said. "You won't think we're overreacting once you've seen her uncle."

"But if she were really in trouble, wouldn't she try to leave, or call her parents, or something?" Jessica asked.

"I don't think she can reach them," Nicholas told her. "She told me her parents are doing research on a Greek island this summer."

"Oh," Jessica said. Her eyes narrowed as they approached Bayview House. "Hey, look at that!

There's a Jaguar parked over there, hidden in the bushes!"

Nicholas followed her gaze. "That's strange," he murmured. "Other than Barbara's uncle's car, which is parked up by the side of the house, I've never seen a car parked here before. I wonder if someone's visiting."

Jessica scrambled out of the Jeep, forgetting the silver-blue Jaguar as she stared up at the magnificent old mansion framed against the evening sky. "What a gorgeous house!" she exclaimed.

"Shh," Nicholas said warningly. "We have to make sure no one sees us." He looked warily back at the Jaguar. "Remember, don't make any noise at all." He pointed. "Look—there's the trail that leads through the woods to the back. We'll let let Barbara know we're here, and she'll come down and meet us."

The twins looked at each other apprehensively, but they turned and followed Nicholas up the narrow path. It was just past seven-thirty, and the summer daylight was beginning to fade. The house and grounds were shrouded in a light mist from the ocean, and it was spooky tiptoeing through the woods single file.

"Come on, you two," Nicholas called in a low voice from up ahead, where the trail ended. "The coast is clear."

Nicholas and the twins ran across a side lawn to the back of the house, which looked out over the cliffs and the sea. Everything was perfectly quiet, except for the sound of the waves. Elizabeth shivered as she looked up at the house. There was just something scary about it. She thought of Barbara, a prisoner inside.

Jessica was shivering, too. "Maybe we shouldn't be here," she said apprehensively.

"Shh," Nicholas said again, putting his finger warningly to his lips. He bent down and scooped up a few pebbles from the ground. "If you two back up a bit, I'll throw these to let her know we're here."

The twins watched as Nicholas took careful aim and threw a small pebble at one of the upstairs windows. Nothing happened, and he aimed and threw again. Then the window opened, and Barbara leaned out, her face flushed and alarmed. "Go back to the woods," she hissed. "Uncle John's downstairs with a visitor. I don't want them to hear you!"

Elizabeth gulped and grabbed Jessica's arm.

"OK, let's go," Nicholas urged, hurrying them back into the woods that bordered on the property of Bayview House. They stood together in the thick shade of the old trees, waiting for Barbara.

"Look, she's coming," Nicholas whispered, seeing her slip out the back door.

Barbara ran on her tiptoes, her long hair flying behind her. She had Rory in her arms. "I'm so sorry, but I was afraid he'd hear us," she murmured as soon as she was near. She looked deeply into Nicholas's eyes before turning to the twins.

"There're two of you!" she exclaimed with a delightful, surprised smile, letting Rory leap out of her arms.

"Barbara, this is my twin sister, Jessica," Elizabeth said.

Barbara managed to be as gracious a hostess outside in the cool woods as she would have been if she were greeting them at her home. "I'm so glad you came," she said simply. "I just wish there was some way I could invite you in."

"Barbara, is everything all right? We've come to help you," Nicholas said, putting his hand on hers.

Barbara blushed at his touch. "I think everything's OK for now. Uncle John has a visitor here tonight. He's been really preoccupied all day. When the visitor comes . . ." She looked uncomfortable, and her voice trailed off.

Elizabeth thought of the silver-blue Jaguar.

58

She wondered if the visitor had come in that car.

"Why don't you come back to Sweet Valley with us and explain the whole thing?" Nicholas asked. "We want to help you, Barbara. If you'd let us take you away from here . . ."

Barbara looked horrified. "I can't possibly leave," she said. "Just think what he might do to Josine if I tried to leave!"

Nicholas looked confused. "But can't you at least tell us what's going on?"

Barbara was about to respond when Rory gave a short, low growl. He was facing the direction of the lawn, where something seemed to be rustling.

"Rory, be quiet," Barbara pleaded, scooping up the terrier.

But the dog struggled wildly in her arms, his hair bristling as he continued to yap. Barbara looked with horror out at the lawn.

"Look," she said, spinning around to face Nicholas and the twins, "you've got to get out of here. Don't stop running till you reach the road. Please," she added, her eyes filling with tears. "Go now, and *run*!"

Elizabeth grabbed Jessica's arm and pulled her with her, stumbling down the trail. Nicholas hung back, looking desperately at Barbara.

But her eyes were like fire. "Go!" she cried again. "Tomorrow night—eight o'clock. Here!" Nicholas whispered urgently. Then he turned and ran after the twins.

"Stop here," he commanded them under his breath when he reached them. He pulled them behind a thick cluster of bushes. They were only yards away from Barbara and could still see and hear her. Elizabeth felt her heart beating fast as they crouched behind the bushes. What if Barbara's uncle found them?

They watched as her uncle stomped into the woods, then grabbed Barbara, twisting her arm roughly and causing her to drop Rory. The terrier snapped at the man's ankles. "What do you think you're doing out here at this time of night?" he demanded.

Barbara, visibly shaken, managed to keep her composure. "I was just taking Rory out, Uncle John."

"You know I've got a guest tonight. And you know you're not supposed to leave your room to walk the dog unless I tell you to."

"Yes, Uncle John," Barbara said quietly, bowing her head. Rory was barking and snarling more furiously than ever. Barbara's uncle, his face contorting with anger, kicked the dog hard. Barbara quickly picked Rory up.

Then Jessica, who had been crouching in an uncomfortable position, lost her balance and slipped. A branch snapped beneath her foot, and the man spun around wildly. Elizabeth's heart was pounding so loudly, she thought it would give them away for sure if the noise didn't. "What's that?" Barbara's uncle cried. "Is someone there?"

The girl looked terrified. "No. It's nothing, Uncle John. It's probably just a squirrel." She looked frantically back at the house, trying to distract him. "But I think your visitor may be leaving. Isn't that him?"

Her uncle stared at her, his jaw tightening. "I told you yesterday when that boy came here, and I'll tell you again. No one comes here to see you, you understand? You know what I'll do if anyone shows up here again?"

"I know," Barbara said sadly, trying to contain the struggling terrier in her arms.

"I can't stand this. I'm going to knock that idiot down," Nicholas hissed, leaping as if he were going to tackle the man.

It took all of Elizabeth's and Jessica's strength to hold him back as Barbara's uncle dragged the helpless, beautiful young girl back to the house with him.

Five

"I wish Nicholas wouldn't go back out to Ronoma alone," Elizabeth said anxiously. It was Tuesday morning, and she and Jessica were seated at their desks, trying to get a good start on the stories they had been assigned the day before. Elizabeth was finding it hard to concentrate. She couldn't seem to keep her mind off what had happened the night before in Ronoma. "But I know nothing I say is going to make any difference," she added. "Wild horses couldn't keep Nicholas away from Bayview House at this point, especially now that he's afraid that that man may be trying to hurt Barbara."

Jessica was looking through a file of material on Paul Lazarow. "You can't really blame him," she murmured. "That guy looked pretty scary.

I'm glad I'm not Barbara. Can you imagine being locked up in that place with only that man and a senile old housekeeper for company?"

"Who said Josine was senile?" Elizabeth demanded.

Jessica shrugged. "I guess Nicholas told me that. Or maybe I just guessed she was." Her eyes narrowed. "It's spooky there, Liz, all that mist and everything. . . ." She sat up straighter. "*I* sure don't want to go back there, *ever*."

Elizabeth bit the end of her pencil. "If only we had more to go on, we could call the police. But right now we have nothing to tell them. So far all we know is that Barbara's uncle—or whatever he is—is treating her roughly. That doesn't seem like much of a police case."

Jessica frowned suddenly at something in her file. "Liz, am I unusually uninformed, or did you ever hear of this guy Paul Lazarow before?"

Elizabeth shook her head. "I have to admit I'm not exactly up on local artists, though."

Jessica flipped back her hair and squinted at the words on the paper. "According to this information, Lazarow was a pretty big deal. He studied in Paris with a lot of famous artists and then came back to his native California hoping to start an artists' colony. It looks like he succeeded, too. He had forty students at one point."

She sighed and closed the folder. "It's kind of romantic, isn't it? Imagine being a wonderful, talented painter."

Elizabeth was intrigued. "What happened to him? It's hard to believe we never heard about a famous artists' colony nearby."

"He died of cancer in 1949," Jessica said. She fiddled with her hairclip. "I wonder what his paintings are like," she added.

Elizabeth rested her chin in her hands. "Well, it sounds like you're making more progress on your story than I am on mine. I've got to find Seth and see if he's got any advice."

Jessica's eyes sparkled. "You're not ready to admit that there's nothing wrong with Russell Kincaid, are you?"

Elizabeth shook her head. "No," she said. "I'm not *that* desperate yet. But I have to admit I'm not coming up with very substantial evidence against him." She looked down at the file she had been poring over. "About the only thing I know for sure is that he made a lot of money very quickly. He and his younger brother were partners for thirty-five years. It looks like they worked mostly in real estate—bought up hotels, some apartment buildings, this big factory in Tijuana. Six months before he announced he was running for mayor, he broke up the partnership." Elizabeth let out a breath. "Not the kind of thing I was hoping to find. I had this idea I would discover some dark secret from his past that would prove that he wouldn't make a good mayor."

"Maybe you'll have to give up and join his campaign," Jessica suggested.

"Forget it, Jess. I'm going to go ask Seth for advice." Elizabeth got to her feet, then looked thoughtfully at her twin. "Do you think I should call Nicholas again before he drives out to Ronoma? I just can't seem to stop worrying about him. The thought of his getting into some kind of awful trouble out there alone . . ."

"I don't see what good worrying is going to do," Jessica said. "Nicholas is a smart guy, Liz. I'm sure he'll be careful." She flipped through her file once more. "Don't you think it's a weird coincidence that Lazarow's artists' colony was in Ronoma?"

"Yeah, it is weird," Elizabeth agreed.

Up until last week, neither of them had ever heard of Ronoma. Now it was suddenly all they talked about!

"I haven't found much either," Seth admitted when Elizabeth told him how frustrating her research on Kincaid was proving so far. "I thought you and I might drive over to Kincaid's campaign headquarters later this afternoon and see if anyone working for him knows more about him that we've been able to find out." He sighed. "Looks to me as if Kincaid has always been pretty good at covering his tracks. I did find two interesting things, though."

He took out an old high school yearbook and showed it to Elizabeth. It was the *Bridgewater Star*, from 1945, the year Kincaid had graduated. "You're not going to believe what it says about our friend the politician and factory owner!" Seth exclaimed. "Look on page thirty-five."

Elizabeth flipped the yearbook open. It took a minute to locate Kincaid's picture. "Gosh, he looks so young!" she exclaimed. Kincaid had been exceptionally good-looking as a boy, with dark, brooding eyes and an expression somewhere between melancholy and anger.

"Read what it says underneath the picture," Seth instructed.

Elizabeth read the print rapidly. "Russell Donovan Kincaid. Favorite author: Hemingway. Ambition: to be a painter." She set the yearbook down. "A painter?" she repeated incredulously.

"That's exactly the reaction I had," Seth said.

"Boy," Elizabeth said, shaking her head. "Who ever would have guessed it?"

"Yeah, it's interesting, but it doesn't tell us much about him. Here's the other thing I found." Seth handed her a faded clipping. "I'm hoping this proves to be a better lead."

Elizabeth examined the clipping with interest. It was a photo of Kincaid with a caption referring to him as an art student. The grainy newspaper photograph showed a still young-looking Russell Kincaid scowling at the camera.

Elizabeth turned it over in her hands. It was dated 1948, but there were no other marks, and no story attached. "Where did you find this?" she asked.

Seth got to his feet. "The newspaper morgue." The morgue was where all the old papers and files were kept. "I couldn't find the rest of the story. But it looks as if Kincaid actually started to fulfill his ambition. He was studying art."

Elizabeth shook her head. "Not exactly the dark secret we were looking for, huh?" she murmured. She pretended to quote a newspaper headline: "Mayoral Candidate Harbors Dream to Paint." She sighed in frustration, then looked again at the photo. There was something so familiar about Kincaid's expression. It reminded her of someone else she had seen recently, but who?

Nicholas had to use a flashlight to find his way from the side of the road through the dense woods to the clearing. It was nearly nine o'clock.

When he finally reached the clearing, it was humming with birds and insects, and the smell of flowers was overpowering. He squinted, trying to guess where in the shadows Barbara might be. Then he saw her emerging from a path across from him. She looked like a vision in a dream. Every time he saw her he had to pinch himself to make sure he was awake. Her dress shone like silver in the twilight. And she had flowers in her hair.

"Barbara!" he said, stepping out of the shadows and putting his hand out.

Then he saw that she had been crying. Her face was completely wet with tears, and her narrow shoulders were trembling.

"Barbara, what is it?" he cried, racing to take her in his arms.

"I was afraid you weren't coming," she said, turning her face up to his. Her lashes were matted with tears, and the expression in her eyes was one of pure anguish.

"Oh, my poor, poor Barbara," Nicholas moaned, holding her tighter and stroking her hair. "I got caught in terrible traffic, and there were some things my mother asked me to do at home. God," he added, frustrated. "If only I could have called you! Then you wouldn't have worried."

Barbara looked stricken. "You can't ever call," she insisted. "You saw how he acted last night! If he knew I'd made friends with you . . ." She took a deep, quavering breath. "Nicholas, I'm honestly not afraid for me. But you and your two friends are in danger now. When you didn't come tonight by eight o'clock, I started to panic. I was so afraid he—" Her voice broke off, and she covered her face with her hands.

Nicholas reached out and touched her wet cheek with the back of his hand. "Oh, Barbara, I'm so happy to see you. Promise me you won't think I'm stupid for saying this, but I think I'm falling in love with you."

Barbara stared at him, her eyelashes still beaded with tears. "I feel the same way," she whispered.

The next minute they were holding each other as if they would never let go. Nicholas could feel her heart pounding next to his. He held her close, still trying to soothe her. "Please," he whispered against her ear. "Tell me what's going

70

on, Barbara. I don't want to pry. You have to tell me."

Barbara shuddered. "I've been having these terrible nightmares," she whispered. "I didn't want to tell you, but . . ." Her voice trailed off again. "But they're getting worse. I have them every night now."

"Tell me," Nicholas said, still holding her. "It'll help for you to describe them."

Barbara drew back from him, her eyes bright with fear. "It's really one nightmare. The same nightmare. I can't remember when I first had it, but I know the first time things were kind of fuzzy, surrounded by mist. I was out on the cliffs, it was night, and there was a cake—a cake with candles," she whispered. "The mist was everywhere. Then there was—him." Her eyes filled with terror. "A man. I couldn't see his face." She was trembling violently now. "He was chasing me. I ran and ran and ran and—" She began to cry again. "Then I got to the edge of the cliff. There was nowhere to go, and I was falling. . . ." She was trembling so hard now, her teeth began to chatter.

"Shh," Nicholas said, stroking her back gently. "It's OK, Barbara. It was only a dream."

"It's the same thing every night now," she whispered. "But it gets clearer and clearer. One night I could see the table out on the patio, set for dinner. The next night I could see the outline of our house. The next night"—she paused and took a deep breath—"I could see his face in the shadows. It was dark and terrible. Then last night I saw the candles more clearly. It was a birthday cake." She shivered. "I think I know why I dreamed about that. My birthday is next Friday. Last week Josine and I talked about it, and she told me that it's the same day as my grandmother's birthday. She acted so frightened, she managed to frighten me. But she wouldn't tell me why. She was so scared." Barbara shook her head, as if she were trying to clear it. "Uncle John is changing, Nicholas. When Josine told him about my birthday, he seemed almost crazy. He shouted at me and told me never to leave the house again unless he said I could. I really think he hates me."

"How could anyone possibly hate you?" Nicholas asked, pulling her closer.

Barbara shook her head. "Sometimes I think he hates me because I remind him of my grandmother. I don't know much about her—only what Josine has been telling me—but there're so many little coincidences. She had a little terrier, too, just like Rory." She sighed. "Maybe that's why he despises Rory so much. He's always threatening to do something awful to him. Anyway, I know that I look like her, too. Sometimes Josine even thinks I'm her. She says things to me that don't make any sense, talks to me about people I don't know. She keeps asking about Jack."

"Josine is very old," Nicholas said gently. "It's very common for people that old to confuse real people with people from the past."

Barbara nodded. "I know that. But I saw a photograph in Josine's bedroom, and I thought it was a picture of me. It turned out to be the other Barbara—my grandmother. It's scary, Nicholas. We look so much alike!" She sighed again. "I know I'm being sensitive, but it's because I've been cooped up here with just the two of them for company. Josine has been talking to me more and more about my grandmother. It's as if she's obsessed. She told me—" She broke off, then seemed to force herself to continue. "Apparently she died in a mysterious accident, out on the cliffs. That's why Josine is so afraid of them."

"I don't understand why your uncle would dislike you just because you remind him of your grandmother," Nicholas mused. "What was his relationship to your grandmother, do you know?"

Barbara shook her head. "I don't know. And I barely know anything about her, just what Josine told me about the accident. She was so young." She shuddered. "I told you before, I hate going up to the cliffs. A few nights ago Uncle John took me up there. He thinks I have a phobia, and he says I need to get over it. It didn't work, though. Being up there with him scared me even more. I saw the place—the place where Josine said she slipped and fell—"

"God, Barbara, he's a sadist!" Nicholas cried, clutching her in his arms. "I want to take you away from him! I can't stand the thought of you having to be here in this house another minute!"

Barbara pulled back a little and held a finger to her lips. "Shh," she whispered, straining to hear over the waves. "Listen, you're not going to be able to stay much longer. If Uncle John notices I'm not in my room, he'll come out searching. And if he finds you . . . Look, I still can't tell you any more than I just did. But you have to believe that I'm not in any real danger here. Uncle John has made that clear to me. The people who are in danger now are you and the twins. Because he thinks you're trying to take me away from here."

"Can't we do *anything*? Can we call the police?"

Barbara was horrified. "Please, Nicholas. Trust

me. Don't do anything at all," she whispered, her face very pale.

"If you knew how it is," he cried out in anguish, "to feel the way I do and watch you suffer."

Barbara put her hand gently on his face. "I know," she said. "Don't you think I know how much I'm making *you* suffer?"

The next minute they were kissing and holding each other tightly.

Finally Barbara pulled away from him. "I have to go," she said sadly.

"Can I see you tomorrow night?"

Barbara nodded. "As long as you promise you'll be careful," she whispered.

Nicholas felt his heart turn over as she slipped her hand from his and ran swiftly across the lawn to the house. If only there was something he could do to help her! There had to be a way.

Nicholas got into his Jeep and turned on the engine. As he rounded a bend in the road, he saw the Jaguar parked just off the side of the road. When he passed it, the car's headlights came on.

The car pulled out and whizzed past, but Nicholas couldn't get a look at the driver. Who would be sitting there that late at night—only to pull out the minute Nicholas got in his car?

He remembered what Barbara had said. She feared that he and the twins could be in danger for trying to interfere.

He wondered if the driver of that silver-blue Jaguar had been following him and waiting to see when he returned to his Jeep. For the rest of the ride home, he couldn't shake the uneasy sensation that someone was watching his every move.

Six

On Wednesday night Nicholas once again went to see Barbara. That visit fell into the same pattern as those of the preceding evenings: He drove to Ronoma as soon as night fell—when her uncle was preoccupied, either with the mysterious visitor who came several evenings a week and whom Barbara had never seen, or with paperwork from his business. "He's such a peculiar man," Barbara confided to Nicholas. "I wish I could learn more about what he does and what his real connection to Bayview House is."

"I thought he was the executor of your grandmother's will," Nicholas said, puzzled.

Barbara confirmed this. "He is. At least, that's what he told my parents. He corresponded with them for months about my visit, and none of us had any question about it then. Josine wrote to my parents, too, saying she really wanted to meet me. She'd been so fond of my grand-mother, and she thought I would love it here. But, Nicholas, the more I hear Josine talk about my grandmother and the past, the less sure I am about anything Uncle John tells me. I know my great-grandfather was an artist. We have some of his paintings in the cellar. Josine showed them to me. That explains why, when my grand-mother died and my mother was just a little baby, she was taken to Europe by the painter DuPres. He must have studied with my great-grandfather. Uncle John told my parents and me that he was my grandfather's cousin." She shook her head. "All I know for sure is that he threatens Josine often. If she weren't so weak and confused, I wouldn't even know that much. But she breaks down sometimes and cries, thinks I'm my grandmother, and complains about him."

Nicholas was growing increasingly distraught about Barbara's safety.

On Thursday, Nicholas met the twins for lunch at a coffee shop near their office. He described to them the claustrophobic atmosphere at Bayview

House, which seemed to be affecting Barbara more and more each day. "I want to help her, but I don't know how," he murmured, barely touching his lunch.

"I think we should get help," Elizabeth said firmly. "Can't we at least try to explain what's going on to the police? Maybe they could send someone out to Bayview House to question Barbara's uncle."

Nicholas shook his head. "I already suggested that. Barbara panicked the minute I mentioned the police." He sighed. "I think I should warn you both. Barbara seems to think that we're in more danger than she is. Whatever it is that her uncle is trying to do, he doesn't want us to interfere."

"Great," Jessica said, shuddering and putting down her fork. "You mean he's going to start following us or something?"

Elizabeth's eyes were wide with alarm. "Nicholas," she cried, "isn't that all the more reason to go to the police? It isn't just us, either. Think about the danger you're in every time you set foot on the property of that house!"

"I have thought about it," Nicholas said quietly. "But I have to see her."

"But, Nicholas—" Jessica started to say.

He cut her off. "Barbara thinks if any of us

tries to involve the police, her uncle will hurt Josine. And who knows what else he might do? It's a risk we just can't take. Not till we can find out more about what's going on there."

Elizabeth was completely mystified. "I just don't understand this, Nicholas. You think her uncle invited Barbara to spend the summer at Bayview House just to torture her? I mean, what's the point? What could he possibly want from Barbara?"

"That's what I want to know, too," Jessica chimed in. "It doesn't make any sense to me. Why is he so scared anyone is going to interfere? What's he trying to hide?"

"That," Nicholas said gravely, "is something I'd like to find out, too. But the way I see it, all I can do for now is go along with what Barbara says." He was pale, and his voice shook.

The twins were quiet, each deep in thought as they finished their lunch and paid the bill. It was almost one o'clock, and they both had to get back to the *News* office.

"Just promise you'll be careful," Elizabeth said when they were on the sidewalk. She and Jessica walked Nicholas to his Jeep.

"Oh, no!" Nicholas exclaimed, reaching up to slip a piece of white paper out from underneath the windshield wiper. "Did I get a ticket?" He studied the paper closely, and suddenly the color drained from his face.

"What is it?" Elizabeth cried.

Nicholas handed her the paper, and Jessica read it over her shoulder. A crude message had been printed in black block letters in the middle of the page: "You'll stay away from Barbara if you know what's good for you. This is your first and last warning."

Jessica let out a gasp and squeezed Elizabeth's arm.

"Nicholas, this is getting to be too—" Elizabeth began, her voice trembling.

"No! Nothing's keeping me away from her," Nicholas interrupted, crumpling up the piece of paper and tossing it into the back of his Jeep. "Nothing—and no one. As long as Barbara's in trouble, I'm going to be there for her. I don't care how dangerous it is."

Nicholas didn't tell Barbara about the warning. Instead, he tried especially hard that evening to cheer her up. She seemed quiet and a little withdrawn, and she admitted that Josine had been frightening her more than usual lately. "I think Josine is having bad memories associated with my birthday," she said slowly.

"The closer it gets, the stranger she acts. Today I was taking Rory for a walk out near the cliffs, and Josine started screaming, 'Don't let her go out there!' Uncle John practically had to restrain her." Barbara shivered. "It's making me really upset," she added, wringing her hands. "I feel like something's going on that everyone around me understands but me."

"And me," Nicholas said, putting his arm around her. "Listen, Barbara. This place is definitely getting to you. You need to get away from here for a while. I'm kidnapping you tomorrow evening and taking you out to dinner." He looked at her with mock fierceness. "OK? I want to take you to the nicest place in all of Ronoma County."

Barbara looked terrified. "How are we going to get away from here without Uncle John knowing?"

"Tell Josine you're sick and going to bed," Nicholas said. "Do you think she'd check up on you?"

"Probably not," Barbara said. "But it's an awfully big chance."

"Can you lock the door?"

"There *is* a key," Barbara said. "One of those old-fashioned ones that fits in a keyhole. I've never tried it, but it would probably work."

"And you can go down the back staircase, the way you usually do, right?"

"Yes, unless someone's in the kitchen. Then I couldn't get out."

"Right. If that happens, just wait for them to leave. I'll be out back, waiting for you—no matter how long it takes." Seeing the fearful expression on Barbara's face, Nicholas said, "It'll be all right. They'll never know you're asleep."

Barbara trembled. "All right," she said at last. "But only for a short time, Nicholas. If he finds out, I'm sure he'll blame it on Josine. It's her job to keep an eye on me. He'll do something dreadful to her if he knows I'm gone."

Nicholas stroked her hand, trying to soothe her. "You really care about Josine, don't you?" he murmured.

Barbara nodded. "I know how much she loved my grandmother," she said softly. "And sometimes I feel like—like she's a child and I have to protect her. If anything happened to her, I'd never forgive myself."

"Nothing will happen," Nicholas assured her. "Just for one evening, I want to take you away from this place. No one will ever know."

Barbara was quiet for a moment. Then a smile broke across her face. "I'm so glad you're here, Nicholas," she whispered. "I feel so safe with you. I don't know what Uncle John wants from me, but as long as you're around, I feel that everything's going to be all right."

There was a restaurant in Denning, the largest town in Ronoma County, that Nicholas thought would be good for dinner: Francesco's, a small, charming Italian restaurant that was perfect for a romantic meal. Everything went just as planned on Friday evening. Barbara got out of the house without her uncle or Josine suspecting anything, and the minute she was in his Jeep Nicholas felt exhilarated, as though he were really rescuing her. They were both elated as they drove into Denning.

"Maybe I should stop for gas now," Nicholas said just before they reached the restaurant. He was afraid the station might close while they were eating.

"Can you fill it up, sir." Nicholas said to the snowy-haired attendant.

The old man nodded. He was about to take the car keys from Nicholas when he caught sight of Barbara and instantly froze. "Barbara," he whispered.

Barbara turned to him quizzically, her beautiful eyes puzzled. "Yes?" she said. "Do I know you?"

A look of terror crossed the old man's face. "Sorry," he said abruptly, still staring at her. "I guess I had you confused with someone else."

Nicholas stared at her. "What was that all about?" he asked as the old man bent to unlock the gas tank on the side of the Jeep.

Barbara looked pale as she fiddled with her bracelet. "I told you how much I look like her," she said. "I think he must have been thinking of my grandmother." She shivered. "He thought I was her, Nicholas. The poor man thinks he's seen a ghost!"

Nicholas cleared his throat. "Barbara," he said finally, "let's promise each other for the rest of the evening we'll forget all about the past. OK? Let's just concentrate on right now. We won't think about anything scary or out of the ordinary."

Barbara bit her lip, her face still slightly pale. "I can't think of anything in the world I'd like better."

A few minutes later Nicholas parked his Jeep in front of Francesco's. He was hurrying around to open the door on Barbara's side when he saw something that made his heart stop.

The silver-blue Jaguar—the same one he had seen parked by the side of the road in front of Bayview House—was parked right in front of him.

"What's wrong?" Barbara asked, taking his arm.

Nicholas stared at the car, swallowing hard. He didn't know what to do. He didn't want to alarm Barbara. Then he remembered what they had just promised each other. He wasn't going to let anything spoil their evening together!

"Nothing," he said, forcing himself to sound natural. But the image of the car stayed in his mind as he followed Barbara into the restaurant. Perhaps, he thought, it was a similar car. But he didn't really believe it. All he could hope was that the person who owned the car didn't recognize Barbara.

"Can I help you?" the maître d' asked, coming forward with a smile.

"My name is Morrow," Nicholas said. "We have a reservation for two."

"Ah, yes," the maître d' said. "Right this way, please." As he led them to a table in the corner, Nicholas glanced out of the corner of his eye and tried to figure out who owned the car. Barbara seemed enchanted with the place. It was warm and homey inside. Each table was covered with a red-and-white-checked cloth and a beautiful centerpiece of fresh flowers. Nicholas was glad she was so taken by the restaurant that she didn't notice the dark-haired man eating alone in the corner across from them. As they approached their table, the man practically jumped to his feet, his face filled with astonishment and alarm as he gaped at Barbara.

Nicholas stared at the man. Was *he* the owner of the Jaguar parked outside?

He looked vaguely familiar to Nicholas. He was a handsome, slightly stocky man in his late fifties or early sixties, his dark hair flecked at the sides with silver, his eyes a steely gray. He was dressed well, in a navy suit. Of all the people in Francesco's, he was the only one eating alone.

Nicholas decided then and there he didn't want Barbara to see the man. After what had happened in the gas station, he didn't want her to be subjected again to the sensation that she was being mistaken for somebody else.

And that was the only possible explanation Nicholas could think of for why this man was staring at Barbara with such a mixture of fascination and horror.

Luckily the maître d' had positioned them so that Barbara was facing the window, her back to the man in the navy suit. He was directly in Nicholas's line of vision, however, and it took incredible self-control for Nicholas to act as if nothing was wrong.

"What a wonderful restaurant!" Barbara exclaimed, opening the menu and smiling. "Nicholas, I can't tell you what a relief it is to be away from that house! I feel like my old self again." She smiled deeply into his eyes. "Only better than my old self, because I'm here with you."

Nicholas did his best to act casual as they decided what to order. But he was painfully aware that everything they did and said was being scrutinized by that man. He hadn't stopped staring at them for a moment since they sat down.

"Is anything wrong?" Barbara asked, putting her hand on his arm.

"No, of course not," Nicholas said, trying to sound calm. "I'm just not used to being with you away from Bayview House, that's all." He smiled at her. "It's going to take me a little while to get used to what a great feeling it is!"

"Me, too," Barbara said. "This is going to be my favorite restaurant on earth from now on," she added.

Nicholas covered her hand with his, trying to ignore the expression on the man's face as he continued to stare. "Barbara," he said, trying to sound casual, "you've never met the visitor who comes to see your uncle, have you?"

Barbara shook her head. "No. Usually when he comes, Uncle John either orders me to go to my room or leave the house. In fact, he some-times tells me to take Rory for a walk—out on the cliffs or somewhere far from the house." She frowned. "I've wondered about him, though. Uncle John almost always acts differently toward me after he's seen him." She tilted her head to one side with a pretty smile. "But you're break-ing the rules! I thought we weren't going to talk about any of that tonight." She clasped his hands tightly and gave him a dazzling smile.

Nicholas smiled back, ignoring the gaze of the strange, intense man on the other side of the restaurant. "You're right," he said. "I prom-ise it won't happen again!"

The rest of the meal turned out to be a lot of fun. They ordered salads and special pasta dishes and took their time, lingering over each course. Nicholas amused Barbara with stories about things that had surprised him when his family first moved to California. And Barbara told him more about her upbringing in Europe. As the child of two university professors, she had trav-eled a great deal. She had grown up speaking English, as well as French, which was why she hardly had an accent. Nicholas could tell how much she loved and respected her parents when she spoke of them. It was also clear how much she missed them, how cut off from them she felt.

But the whole time they were talking, Nicholas was still watching the man on the other side of the restaurant. Clearly he was flustered and upset. Once he knocked over his wineglass, and Nicholas could see his hands were trembling badly. Finally—after what seemed to Nicholas like forever—the man called for the check. But once he had paid, he seemed reluctant to go. He walked to the door slowly, never taking his eyes off Barbara.

Nicholas breathed a sigh of relief when the man was gone. At last he could relax and enjoy the meal!

Their conversation was easy and comfortable, and Nicholas found himself thinking how much he enjoyed her company. "I can't ever remember a dinner this nice," he said softly.

"Me, either," Barbara said, her eyes fixed on his. "It's the nicest time I've had since I came to California."

"You know," he said, after they had ordered dessert, "we have to figure out what we're going to do on your birthday. It's only a week away. First you have to tell me what you want for a present, and then what you want to do more than anything else that night."

Barbara paled slightly. "Oh, Nicholas, I don't know. I've been trying not to think about it too much because every time I do, I remember that nightmare, and how strangely Josine acts about the whole thing."

Nicholas put his hand over hers again. "I want it to be a special night for you," he said tenderly. "You've had so much anxiety and worry since you've been here. On your birthday everything should be perfect."

Barbara bit her lip. She suddenly looked sad. "I don't think we have much choice," she said. "I can't invite you to the house. And you know there's no way I can leave. I think we'll just have to try to meet each other in the woods next to the house, like we've been doing."

"It's so frustrating!" Nicholas burst out. "I want to make it the best night in the world for you. I'd love to take you out—to the ballet, to a concert, somewhere in L.A.—anywhere. . . ."

But Barbara was shaking her head with her usual gentle smile. "You don't understand," she murmured. "Much as I'd love to be able to do what I please, I don't need to go anywhere special for our time together to be wonderful." She pressed his hand gently. "The best thing in the world for me is just to be with you." She lowered her eyes. "And to know you're safe," she added softly.

Nicholas wondered if he had made a mistake

in bringing up her birthday. Clearly it upset her to think about it. And all he wanted to do was make her happy.

"We won't plan anything yet," he said. "Let's just wait and see. Who knows what'll happen by next week?"

Barbara didn't respond, but a flicker of sadness crossed her face.

Later, after Nicholas had paid their check, he helped Barbara back into the Jeep and started the motor. "I wish so much I didn't have to take you back there!" he cried.

"I know. It's hard," Barbara whispered. "If it weren't for Josine and Rory— Oh, Nicholas, wouldn't it be wonderful if I never had to go back there?"

"I'm going to find a way to rescue you," Nicholas said grimly, turning the Jeep onto the main road that ran through Denning.

Neither of them said much on the trip back. They were both dreading the end of the evening. Nicholas drove more and more slowly as they got closer to Bayview House.

It was dark now, and he turned his lights off so he could pull over to the side of the road without anyone knowing his Jeep was there. "Will you be all right?" he asked her softly, cradling her face in his strong hands.

Barbara nodded, her eyes big and sad. "Thank you for tonight," she whispered. "It was absolutely wonderful."

"I'll be back tomorrow," he promised her, bending down to brush her lips with his.

She stiffened slightly. "Just remember—be careful," she cried softly. She opened the door and slipped out of the Jeep, quietly making her way to the trail that led through the woods to the house.

Nicholas's heart ached as he watched her go. Then, sighing heavily, he turned the ignition back on and flipped on his headlights.

He couldn't believe what he saw in front of him. Bathed in the reflected lights from his headlights, the silver-blue Jaguar was parked by the side of the road—*empty*. Where was the driver? And what was his connection to Bayview House, and to Barbara?

Seven

Jessica slept late on Saturday morning. By the time she came downstairs, both of her parents were out doing errands. Steven and Adam were playing tennis, and Elizabeth was outside by the pool, engrossed in the morning paper.

Jessica poured herself a bowl of cereal and some juice and wandered out to the backyard. She plopped down on one of the patio chairs and ate her breakfast in silence, staring out at the shimmery pool.

"What's wrong?" Elizabeth asked her at last, putting down the paper.

Jessica shook her head. "I had a really scary dream last night," she said finally. "It was at Bayview House. You were there, and so was Nicholas, but we couldn't find Barbara." She sighed. "We were running through the woods, calling her name, and Nicholas was totally hysterical. He was in front, running the fastest." She shuddered. "Then he tripped and fell over something, and I looked down to see what made him trip—it was a body!" She pushed her cereal bowl aside. "I woke up in a sweat and couldn't remember where I was or anything."

"Poor Jess," Elizabeth said. "That sounds awful."

"Maybe I shouldn't have gone with Lila to see that horror movie last night," Jessica said faintly. The nightmare had obviously really gotten to her.

Suddenly Elizabeth sat up straight. "Don't say anything else. It looks like we have company —and company who probably won't want to hear about your nightmare!"

Nicholas Morrow, a worried expression on his face, was crossing the lawn.

"Hi, guys," he said, sitting down on a patio chair and facing them gravely. "I tried ringing the door bell, and when no one answered, I thought I'd see if you were out here. I really wanted to talk to you. Last night—" He stopped in midsentence when he caught sight of the front page of the newspaper. "Liz, who's that guy?"

He was staring at the picture of Russell Kincaid under the headline: "Candidates Step Up Campaign as Election Approaches."

"That guy?" Elizabeth echoed incredulously. "Nicholas Morrow, don't tell me you don't know who Russell Kincaid is! You must be the only person in Sweet Valley who hasn't seen his picture plastered all over the papers."

Nicholas was pale. "I haven't looked at a newspaper in ages," he whispered. He was transfixed by the photograph.

"What is it, Nicholas?" Jessica demanded.

Nicholas ran his fingers through his hair in a nervous gesture. "You're not going to believe this, but I think Russell Kincaid is the owner of the Jaguar we saw parked by the side of the road near Bayview House."

Elizabeth wrinkled her brow. "I don't get it. What would Russell Kincaid be doing at Bayview House?"

"That's what I'd like to know," Nicholas said grimly. "And that isn't all." After taking a deep breath, he proceeded to tell the twins what had happened the night before at Francesco's.

"You mean Kincaid was eating dinner there?" Jessica asked him.

Nicholas nodded. "Only I didn't know it was Kincaid. He was eating alone. The only thing I

97

recognized was his car, which was parked outside. You should have seen the way he reacted to Barbara, though."

"Barbara?" Elizabeth repeated, her eyes wide. "How could he possibly know Barbara?"

"I haven't the faintest idea," Nicholas replied. "All I know is that he looked absolutely horrified when he saw her. He almost jumped out of his chair, and even though her back was to him, he kept trying to catch glimpses of her throughout our whole meal like she—" He shook his head. "Like she was a ghost," he finished miserably.

Jessica looked from Nicholas to her sister with alarm. "This is really starting to freak me out," she said in a low voice.

"It *is* strange," Elizabeth said, frowning at the newspaper picture as if the answer lay there. "So what happened? Did he try to speak to Barbara? Did she recognize him, too?"

"No. The way we were seated, she couldn't see him. To tell you the truth, I don't think she noticed him at all. And he didn't come over or try to talk to her."

"Maybe she looks like someone he knows," Elizabeth suggested, trying as hard as she could to come up with a reasonable explanation. "What was Kincaid doing in Ronoma County, anyway?"

"I haven't told you the part that really scared me yet," Nicholas continued, rubbing the back of his neck and sighing. "I told you I've seen this car out at Bayview House before, and not just the night you guys were there with me, right?"

The twins nodded.

"Well, when I took Barbara back to the house, the Jaguar was there again. There was no mistaking it."

Elizabeth stared at him. "That's incredible," she said. Now that reasonable explanations seemed unlikely, she was beginning to get alarmed. "Why would Kincaid be going to Bayview House?"

"That's what I want to figure out," Nicholas cried. He jumped out of the chair and paced nervously back and forth in front of the twins. "I think he must be the visitor Barbara keeps talking about who comes to see her uncle. But why? What can he possibly be doing out there?"

Elizabeth and Jessica stared at each other. Neither had any idea at all what to say to their distraught friend.

"I was upset before I knew who this guy was," Nicholas admitted. "But now that I know it's Russell Kincaid, I'm really confused!" He stared at them helplessly. "You guys, something weird is going on. I'm afraid if I can't do something to help Barbara, she may be caught in the middle of a horrible situation she can't escape from."

Nicholas took a deep breath. He hadn't been to Bayview House in the daytime since the day after he'd first met Barbara, the day after the *News* picnic.

Barbara had warned him never to come before night. It was too dangerous, she said. Her uncle was almost always somewhere nearby, and in broad daylight, hiding would be impossible.

But Nicholas had to see her. Immediately. And his parents had asked him to go out with friends of theirs that evening. There was no way he could call Barbara or get a message to her. No, the only thing to do was to risk it.

He parked his Jeep on the shoulder of the road and peered up at the house, which looked, from this vantage point, so beautiful and unthreatening, it was hard to believe it could be concealing sinister secrets. It was a gorgeous, sparkling-clear day, and Nicholas felt his spirits lift a little. Maybe everything would be all right after all.

He crossed the road and started up the trail

through the woods, walking on tiptoe so he wouldn't snap a twig or make any noise. Then he realized his precautions didn't seem warranted. No one was around. The grounds and house seemed completely deserted.

Checking carefully to make sure the coast was clear, Nicholas darted from the woods to the back of the house. Scooping up a handful of pebbles, he aimed expertly at Barbara's window.

After a minute the window opened, and Barbara looked out. "Nicholas!" she hissed, her face drained of all color. "What are you doing here?"

"Please come down," he called softly. "I know you told me not to come, but I had to see you!"

She looked behind her, her face filled with terror. "I'll be down in a few minutes. Meet me in the woods," she whispered. "And *watch out!*"

Nicholas looked around furtively, but he didn't see any sign of Barbara's uncle. Still, he didn't want to distress Barbara. He slipped back into the woods and waited impatiently for her to arrive.

It was almost ten minutes before she came down. For the first time Barbara was wearing jeans, rather than the old-fashioned dresses Nicholas had gotten used to seeing her in. Her hair was tied back, and her eyes were red from crying.

"What is it? What's wrong?" he cried in alarm, throwing his arms around her.

Barbara shook her head and wiped a tear from the corner of her eye. "It's Rory. He wasn't here when I got home last night, and he's been missing ever since. Nicholas, I think Uncle John has found out about us. I think he knows that I snuck out last night, and he's trying to punish me."

"He wouldn't hurt Rory, would he?" Nicholas demanded.

"I don't know, Nicholas. I just don't know." Barbara buried her face in her hands. "My poor little puppy. I should never have brought him with me. I should have let my parents take him with them. But I couldn't bear to leave him behind, and now he's gone!"

"Don't cry," Nicholas said soothingly, holding her close to him. "We'll find Rory, I promise."

Barbara looked up, her cheeks stained with tears. "Nicholas, it's becoming too dangerous for us to see each other anymore. I think Uncle John is trying to warn us—both of us." She gulped hard. "Don't you see what he's doing? He knows how much I love Rory—that's why he's taken him." She looked away, unable to meet his eyes. "The next thing he'll try to do is hurt you," she whispered. "Don't you see, Nicholas? You have to protect yourself! You just can't come here anymore!"

"Barbara," Nicholas said, engulfing her in his arms, "you know me well enough by now to know I can't stay away from you. And, anyway, even if I did, it wouldn't change your situation. I'll do anything else you'll let me do to help you, but you can't stop me from coming to see you." He brushed her damp hair back from her face.

"What if I said I don't want you to come anymore?" Barbara asked, staring up at him, her lower lip trembling.

"Forget it," Nicholas said, the tenderness in his voice making the phrase sound almost gentle. He leaned down to kiss her, and when he pulled back, his eyes were filled with tears.

Barbara took a deep, quivering breath. "OK," she said at last. "But at least promise me you won't come back during the day anymore. Uncle John's out this afternoon, but Josine's here. If she saw you and told him. . . ." She shook her head.

"I thought Josine was on your side," Nicholas said, perplexed.

"Josine's so old," Barbara said wearily, "I

103

don't think she's really aware of what's going on all the time. Most of the time she thinks I'm my grandmother. This morning she came in and tried to give me a pair of cuff links. She kept saying, 'They're Jack's. I saved them for you.' When I asked her who Jack was, she started to cry, and she kept mumbling, 'He needs you, Barbara. You're all he ever had.' "

"Wow, that sounds pretty frightening," Nicholas said.

"It was," Barbara confirmed. "The strange thing is that she'll be fine for hours, sometimes even days. And then something seems to remind her of the past, and she slips back into another world." She brushed a stray hair off her face. "My birthday is really upsetting her. She keeps following me around with a haunted look on her face, crying." Barbara shivered. "Something terrible must have happened to my grandmother the night of her birthday. Josine won't tell me what it is, but the way she cries and throws her arms around me, I'm sure of it. She begs me to stay away from the cliffs, tells me she has to protect me."

"Barbara, I can't stand thinking of you trapped here with Josine and your uncle," Nicholas cried in a tortured voice. "Please, please let me call the police! Or at least just leave here with me."

Barbara shook her head. "It would never work," she said faintly. "I told you. If I left—if I ran away, I know he'd harm Josine. I can't leave her! For now, just be patient, please, Nicholas. And try to protect yourself. I promise you, I'm doing the best I can to protect *me*."

Nicholas had to agree.

"Let's try to find Rory," Barbara added disconsolately. "Maybe he just ran away." She reached into her pocket and took out a small foil-wrapped packet. "I brought some of his favorite biscuits. If we find him—"

"We'll find him," Nicholas said, trying to sound more confident than he felt.

For the rest of the afternoon, Nicholas and Barbara combed the extensive property around Bayview House, trying to find the little terrier. They looked everywhere—in the woods, in the garden—but found no Rory.

"Rory! Here, Rory!" Barbara called sadly, clapping her hands. There was no response.

"What's that?" Nicholas asked, pointing to a small structure several hundred yards to the east of the house.

"Oh, that's where my great-grandfather used to paint." Barbara flipped back her ponytail. "It's all locked up now. Josine has a key, but she won't let me in. She cried when I asked her

if I could see my great-grandfather's studio."
She sighed. "Poor Rory. Nicholas, I think Uncle
John must have him."

"We haven't looked up there," Nicholas said,
pointing to the cliffs behind the house.

A strange expression crossed Barbara's face.
"I don't really want to go up there," she whispered. But the next minute she realized that she
had to. "You're right, Nicholas. Rory could have
gotten trapped on one of those ledges. Let's
go." And without a backward glance she headed
for the loamy path leading out to the cliffs.

Nicholas admired the grace with which she
handled the steep path. Bayview House hung
right over the sea. There was no beach below it,
just the sharp rocks of the cliffs, leading down
to the water. A narrow sandy trail ran right
along the edge of the highest cliff, and it was
there that they walked.

Nicholas shivered. It was so wild and lonesome up there, he thought, with the wind blow-
ing the loam and the waves pounding below
them in a foamy frenzy.

But he forgot his own fear the next minute
when Barbara let out a thin, horrible cry.

"What is it?" he demanded, racing up to join
her.

She had dropped to her knees, and big tears

106

were rolling down her cheeks. She was staring at a small band of leather laying on the path.

"It's Rory's collar," she said, picking it up. "It's Uncle John," Barbara cried, rocking back and forth on her knees, the tiny collar clasped to her chest. "Don't you see, Nicholas? He's trying to warn us both!"

Nicholas tried to put his arms around her, but she was sobbing so violently, he couldn't hold her. He felt his own heart beating loudly.

Right then Nicholas hated Barbara's uncle more than he'd ever known he could hate another human being. He didn't know how anyone could hurt an innocent creature like Rory.

But behind his anger another emotion loomed even larger. Standing up there on those rocky cliffs, Nicholas knew, for the first time in his life, what it meant to be really and truly frightened. And not just for Barbara, but also for himself.

"Are you going to be all right?" Nicholas asked Barbara as she walked with him through the woods to the Jeep.

Barbara nodded. "I'm going to try," she whispered. "Listen, Nicholas, I want you to stay away from here for a few days. Just give me a chance to let things settle down." She shivered. "After what's happened, I feel I can't risk letting you come back until things are calmer. I just have no idea what he might do to you."

Nicholas kicked at a root. "What if I come back with the twins? How would that be?"

Barbara sighed deeply. "I don't know if it would be better or worse. You might be safer, but then they'd be in danger." She shook her head. "Just give it a couple of days. Wait and come Tuesday. That's only three days away. By then . . ."

Nicholas fumbled for his car keys, which were in the pocket of his jeans. He didn't see how he was going to be able to stand not seeing her for three days.

He was about to protest again when he stopped short, his mouth dropping open. They had just come out of the woods, and Nicholas could see his Jeep.

"Oh, no!" Barbara cried, covering her eyes.

The tires had been slashed to ribbons and the windshield cracked into a thousand little slivers.

Neither of them spoke for a minute.

"What will you do?" Barbara asked, her eyes dark with fear.

"I'll hitchhike to Denning and call a tow truck,"

Nicholas said, looking incredulously at the damaged vehicle.

Barbara buried her face in her hands. "I'm such a fool," she whispered. "How can I possibly think you'll be safe if you stay away from here? Now that he knows you and your car—now that he knows you're trying to help me. . . ." She shook her head in despair. "You aren't going to be safe anywhere anymore, Nicholas. And neither are the twins!"

Eight

The Sweet Valley Art Museum was a small modern building set in a breathtaking spot overlooking the ocean. Palm trees lined the walkway leading up to the front entrance, and when the twins parked the Fiat in the lot on Monday afternoon and started up the walkway, they saw a bright red banner over the front door that read: Paul Lazarow: A Retrospective.

"I can't remember the last time I was here," Elizabeth said. "I'm glad you talked me into coming with you, Jess. This is a great way to spend a lunch hour."

"What time did Nicholas say he was meeting us?" Jessica asked, looking around the parking lot. The Jeep was nowhere to be seen.

"I think about one. It's ten till now," Elizabeth answered, glancing at her watch.

"Well, let's go in and look around. He'll find us inside," Jessica said. As the twins crossed the parking lot to the museum entrance, Jessica dug around in her pocketbook for her notebook.

"Liz, I can't seem to find out any details about this artist's life." Jessica extracted the notebook and her pencil. "I mean, I know the basic facts: born in 1895, studied in France with a couple of great artists, bought a place in Ronoma, married, had one daughter who died young. He died a few years after she did. That's it. Even the catalog accompanying the exhibition has no other facts."

"You checked the newspaper morgue, didn't you?" Elizabeth asked her as they entered the museum.

Jessica looked sheepish. "Well, not exactly. Dan gave me a file, and I thought that was all there was."

Elizabeth looked at her sister with disbelief. "Jess, Dan probably got that material from the morgue, since that's where all the old clippings are kept. But you've got to go back and check the files again. He may have missed something, or sometimes things get misfiled. Doing research is like being a detective. You can't overlook anything."

Jessica sighed. "All right, all right. I guess I can go back and do some more research after we look at the paintings."

"There are a lot more paintings than I thought there'd be," Jessica said, looking with consternation down the long gallery.

Elizabeth grinned. "It won't be that bad," she tried to assure her. "It can't hurt us to get a little culture."

"I wish Nicholas would get here," Jessica said anxiously, moving closer to examine the first painting. It was called "Seaside." Lovely blues and greens dominated the canvas, and Elizabeth admired the stormy aspect of the sea that the artist had captured.

Elizabeth glanced at her watch again. "It's only a minute after one. He's not really very late yet." She moved away from her sister to admire the next painting while Jessica hunched down to scrawl some notes.

"I'm going to walk around and look at everything once first," Elizabeth told Jessica, "and then come back and start over." Jessica, intent on her note-taking, didn't respond. The gallery was empty except for the guard, standing quietly in one corner, so Elizabeth could browse as she pleased.

She liked Lazarow's work very much, she discovered. The paintings were divided into three groups: Paris, Brittany, and Ronoma, the three places Lazarow had spent most of his time. The Ronoma paintings were last, and Elizabeth hadn't reached them yet when she saw Nicholas stroll into the gallery. She decided to start over and look at the paintings with him.

"Hi!" she said brightly, hurrying over to meet him.

Nicholas smiled briefly at her, but he didn't look too happy. In fact, he looked considerably worse than he had in days. There were dark shadows under his eyes, and he seemed agitated and ill at ease.

"What's wrong?" Elizabeth asked.

Nicholas ran his hand through his hair. "Liz, I'm worried."

Elizabeth glanced around to make sure no one was within earshot. Jessica hurried over just as she urged, "Tell me what's going on."

Nicholas took a deep breath. "OK. But you're going to be pretty shocked. I know I was. I think Barbara's uncle found out that I helped her sneak out of the house on Friday night. Because Saturday, when I went out there—"

His voice broke. "It was absolutely terrible. Her little dog, Rory, was missing. We ended up searching all over the place for him." He couldn't look the twins in the eyes. "Finally we went up to the cliffs, and we found—"

"Don't say it," Jessica said, gasping.

Nicholas's eyes darkened with fear and anger as he remembered the scene. "Rory's collar was lying right there on the rocks. That creep left it there for Barbara to find. I didn't think she'd ever stop crying."

"But why would he do something like that?" Elizabeth cried.

"That's what's scaring me." Nicholas shifted his weight, glancing nervously around him. "He's warning us, I think. And not just Barbara." He told them what had happened to his Jeep. "Barbara thinks we're all in danger. Not just her, but the three of us, too."

Jessica's eyes were huge. "You mean he slashed the tires on your Jeep? How'd you get out of there?"

"It wasn't easy. I ended up having to walk most of the way to Denning because I had trouble getting someone to pick me up. Then I had to have it towed. I got new tires easily enough, but it's going to take awhile to get the windshield repaired." He shook his head. "The Jeep can be fixed, but that doesn't help us locate Barbara's dog."

"And Barbara really thinks it's a warning?" Elizabeth asked.

Nicholas nodded. "She made me promise not to go see her until tomorrow." He bit his lip. "And I was wondering if you guys—"

Jessica went pale. "You mean, Nicholas, you want us—"

Elizabeth took a deep breath. "I think we all need to calm down," she said. She put her hand on Jessica's arm. "Let's look around at the paintings," she added, trying hard to keep her fear from showing. "Come on, Nicholas. We all need to take our minds off this. Let's just try to relax for half an hour or so and then figure out what we're going to do next."

"You're right," Nicholas said, looking at the paintings around him. "Maybe it'll help. But I feel like she's all I can think about."

Elizabeth steered him to the first painting. "Just take it easy. We're not going to leave Barbara out at Bayview House alone." She glanced briefly at Jessica, then away. "If you want us to come out with you tomorrow, we will."

Jessica turned white. "Uh—yeah, Nicholas,"

she managed to choke out. "If you really need us—I mean—"

Over the next fifteen minutes, Nicholas calmed down considerably. They moved from painting to painting, making brief comments about the color or composition. "These paintings seem so familiar, but I don't really know how I could have seen them before," Nicholas murmured, stopping to reexamine "Seaside."

Elizabeth had moved ahead to the first of the Ronoma paintings, which she hadn't looked at yet. She gazed admiringly at the first full-sized painting of a lovely summer landscape. It was called "Artist's Studio."

Nicholas stopped short when he came up beside her. "Liz," he said excitedly, grabbing her arm. "That's the studio at Bayview House!"

"Are you sure?" Elizabeth asked, her brow wrinkling.

Jessica had moved ahead to the next painting, and all of a sudden she let out a soft cry. "You guys," she said emphatically. "Come here!"

Nicholas and Elizabeth hurried over to join Jessica. She was standing in front of a large canvas illuminated from above by a museum light. It was the largest canvas in the room, and the most beautiful.

Next to the painting a small plaque read,

"Artist's Daughter." It was dated 1948. In the painting a strikingly beautiful girl gazed out from her perch on a garden bench, her long, chestnut-colored hair hanging smoothly to her waist. A little dog was curled in her lap, and one of her hands rested gently on its neck, as if to soothe it. Her eyes seemed so bright and lifelike, it was as if she were about to speak.

No one said a word. They stood perfectly still, staring at the painting, their eyes wide with amazement. Nicholas was incredibly pale, and the twins could hear him breathing heavily.

Finally Jessica broke the silence. "It doesn't make sense," she said fearfully.

Nicholas didn't take his eyes off the portrait for a moment. "I can't believe it," he whispered. "It's her! Every last tiny detail—the necklace she wears, the straw hat next to her, her blue dress—even Rory. . . ."

"Nicholas, you're scaring me," Elizabeth said, her voice shaking.

"It's Barbara," Nicholas said weakly. "But how—?"

"You'd better sit down," Elizabeth said, noticing again how pale he was. She was afraid he was going to faint.

Nicholas shook his head. He scrutinized the painting, his eyes running from one detail to the next as though he couldn't believe what he saw before him. He reread the small plaque beside the painting.

Elizabeth put her hand on his arm. She could feel him trembling. "Look," she said nervously, "there has to be a logical explanation. We all know she looks like Barbara, but—"

Nicholas shook his head. "She *is* Barbara! But that painting was done forty years ago. How could—?" He couldn't finish his question.

"Listen," Elizabeth said, trying to calm all of them down. "Didn't you say that Barbara looked very much like her grandmother? This must be her. Paul Lazarow's daughter is—I mean, was—Barbara's grandmother." She calculated quickly. "The dates are right," she added.

Nicholas didn't say anything at first. "Liz," he finally managed, "we have to find out everything we can about Paul Lazarow's daughter."

"Why?" Jessica cried. "What good will that do?"

Nicholas shook his head slowly, still transfixed by the portrait. "Something happened to Barbara's grandmother that's scaring everyone at the house half to death. I don't know why or how, but I know that's part of the reason her uncle brought Barbara back here. It's why she's so frightened at the thought

119

of her birthday. Her birthday happens to be the same as her grandmother's. And her grandmother *died* on her birthday."

"You sound awfully suspicious, Nicholas. What do you think happened?" Elizabeth asked.

"I think someone murdered her," Nicholas said. "And whoever did must be trying to harm Barbara, too!"

Half an hour later Nicholas and the twins were back in the newsroom office. Nicholas had taken a cab over to the museum. On the way back to the *News*, they squeezed him into the back of the Fiat.

"I warned you, Nicholas," Jessica said. "I haven't been able to find out very much about Paul Lazarow. I mean, you're welcome to whatever I've got. But so far it's all pretty sketchy."

Nicholas shook his head. "It just seems like finding out more about the way Barbara's grandmother died may prove the only clue."

Elizabeth nodded. "I think you're right," she said.

But Jessica looked unnaturally pale. "I don't like it," she murmured. "How come Barbara looks exactly like her grandmother, down to things like jewelry and clothes? And what about having the same birthday?" She shivered.

"Jessica—" Elizabeth began warningly.

But Jessica's alarm seemed to heighten as the three of them began digging through back files in the newspaper's morgue.

"You guys," she said, her voice low, "I found something. It's under 'Barbara Lazarow.' "

"What is it? Is it about her grandmother? Let me see it!" Nicholas shouted, practically snatching the article out of her hands.

"Here," she said, passing him a yellowed clipping. "This is what the *News* ran when Lazarow's daughter died."

Nicholas took the clipping from her. "Barbara Lazarow, the only child of the renowned painter Paul Lazarow, was tragically drowned last Friday. An inquest is being held in the Ronoma County Court a week from today. Lazarow has refused to comment on either the accident itself or the inquest. The night of the accident, July 28, was Barbara Lazarow's twenty-first birthday."

Elizabeth and Jessica stared at each other. Nicholas read and reread the article, the clipping trembling in his hands.

"I can't stand it," Jessica moaned. "She's got the same name as her grandmother *and* the same birthday. You guys, this is *weird!* I think Barbara is a ghost!"

Nicholas turned absolutely white.

"Don't be ridiculous, Jess," Elizabeth said staunchly. "Barbara isn't a ghost. We were all out there together. We all saw her, remember? She's flesh and blood, just like we are."

Nicholas didn't say anything, but he was clearly shaken.

"Let's just keep searching," Elizabeth said, giving her twin a stern look. "We're bound to find something else useful if we keep looking under other categories."

For the next few minutes the three worked in silence, combing through the files. Finally Elizabeth found something of interest.

"Local Artist Starts Colony for Students," the headline ran.

"Hey, here's something else on Lazarow!" she cried, reading rapidly to herself. Then she began to paraphrase the article for Nicholas and Jessica.

"Apparently Paul Lazarow bought the summer house in Ronoma for two reasons. First, so his daughter could spend summers in California, where Lazarow himself was raised and where he felt he really belonged. And second, because he wanted to start an artists' colony, very much like the one where he had studied in Paris. He was to be the master teacher, and he wanted to get the best possible students to study with him."

"That all makes sense," Nicholas said, nodding. He narrowed his eyes then. "Liz, what's wrong?" he demanded, seeing the distraught expression on her face.

"Well, look—there's a photograph here, taken in"—Elizabeth squinted down at the date—"the fall of 1947. The year before Barbara's death." She shook her head, staring at it. "It's a photograph of Lazarow with two of his students. You're not going to believe this in a million years. One of them is Russell Kincaid."

"Let me see!" Jessica cried, grabbing the clipping.

Elizabeth was absolutely right. The man in the photograph was Kincaid. He looked about twenty.

"Wow," Jessica said. "What was *he* doing studying with Paul Lazarow?"

"Good question," Elizabeth admitted, still scrutinizing the photograph. "Seth found Kincaid's yearbook, and apparently his ambition in high school was to become a painter." She sighed and set the clipping down. "Nicholas," she said slowly, "I wonder if any of this helps explain why Kincaid looked so shocked when he saw Barbara the other night in that restaurant in Denning. Do you suppose he could have known her grandmother? If the resemblance between them is so strong that it's got all three of us freaked out . . ."

Nicholas had taken the clipping from Jessica and was staring at the photograph of Kincaid. "Yes," he agreed. "If Kincaid knew Barbara Lazarow, that would explain what happened the other night. But I wonder how well he knew her. And was he her friend—or her enemy? In either case, why is he hanging around Ronoma now, unless there's something he wants from *this* Barbara!"

Nine

"OK, you guys," Nicholas whispered. "Let's go over the plan one more time." It was Tuesday night, and he and the twins were sitting in his Jeep with the headlights off, trying to get their courage up to sneak through the woods to Bayview House. "First of all, remember, we have to be as quiet as possible, right?"

"Sure," Jessica mumbled. Elizabeth just nodded.

"The plan is to sneak up behind the house and get Barbara's attention by throwing pebbles." Nicholas cleared his throat. "But if anyone comes out—if you see her uncle *any*where— just run back to the Jeep as fast as you can." He looked at them, his eyes grave. "I'm going to put the keys under the floor mat. If something happens to one of us"—he paused and swallowed hard—"the others can still get away and get help. All right?"

Elizabeth could feel her heart pounding loudly. Bayview House was barely visible in the mist that had rolled up from the sea. "Nicholas, we can still go back and get help now," she said, trying to keep the fear out of her voice. "There's no reason—"

"We can't do that, Liz," Nicholas interrupted. "You know that." He opened the door of the Jeep. "Come on," he added.

Elizabeth and Jessica turned to look at each other. "Be careful, Jess," Elizabeth whispered, squeezing her sister's hand. She felt a sudden pang. She had dragged her twin into this whole mess. If she hadn't invited Nicholas to the company picnic, none of them would be here now.

Jessica squeezed back, trying to look brave. A twig snapped. She jumped and grabbed her sister's arm. "What was that?"

"Just Nicholas," Elizabeth assured her. "Come on, Jess. Let's go." With that the twins slid out of the Jeep and followed Nicholas, creeping behind him single file up toward the house.

"What's taking so long?" Jessica whispered several minutes later. The first pebble hadn't worked, and neither had the next few. Nicholas and the twins were huddled out behind the house, shivering with fear. The evening air had grown cool from the ocean breeze.

"She's got to be in there. She knew we were coming tonight," Nicholas said, frowning.

The third attempt to get Barbara's attention failed, too.

"Nicholas, we'd better go," Elizabeth said uneasily. The wind was picking up, and it was hard to tell if she was hearing something in the distance, or if it was just the wind.

"I've got to see her," Nicholas cried brokenly.

"Come on," Jessica pleaded, tugging at his hand. "We tried, Nicholas." When his expression darkened, she added, "We'll come back tomorrow night. But let's not hang around here now!"

Finally Nicholas relented. There was nothing else he could do.

They had tiptoed halfway down the path in the woods when Nicholas grabbed Elizabeth's arm. "Be quiet," he commanded them. "I hear something—up ahead—in the clearing!"

Elizabeth turned to face Jessica, her eyes wide with terror. Sure enough, she could hear the murmur of voices.

"Stay close," Nicholas whispered. He edged forward, then peered around a tree at the scene before him. The twins moved up close enough

127

to see, letting the thick foliage screen them from view.

It was Barbara—and the old housekeeper, Josine.

Barbara was dressed in a filmy, ice-blue, old-fashioned dress. Her long hair was loose, and she looked beautiful in the moonlight. Tears glistened on her face as she turned toward Josine. "I don't think I can bear it anymore," she wept. "Josine, you must know why he treats me so meanly."

The snowy-haired housekeeper looked at her with a tender expression. "Poor Barbara. Didn't I warn you that he hated Jack? I thought I told you. But you were so stubborn . . ."

"Josine," Barbara said, sobbing, falling down on her knees and clasping the housekeeper as if she could shake sense into her. "It's me, Barbara. I'm her granddaughter. Not her. Don't you understand?" She wiped the tears from her eyes. "I know he deliberately confuses you, making me dress like my grandmother, telling you things—but, Josine," she pleaded, "try to understand. Try to help me!"

Josine's eyes filmed over. "I told you it would never work," she mused softly. "Trying to hide the baby—Jack's baby—from him. I told you to leave the country. Didn't I? Didn't I tell you that hate can be as powerful as love sometimes?"

What kind of strange story was Josine trying to tell Barbara? Everything about the scene was so mysterious: Barbara's filmy dress from another period, the moonlight, the urgency in her face, and Josine's vague insistence on talking about an era long passed.

Then suddenly the old woman's mood seemed to change. "Listen," she hissed. "You want to know what happened to your grandmother, don't you? You with all your questions. Well, I'll tell you, child. She didn't fall on those cliffs. She was *pushed*. You understand? Murdered."

Barbara stared at her, her eyes filling with horror. "But, Josine, who—"

"Murdered," Josine repeated, almost mesmerized. "I'm warning you," Josine added. "Be careful. And keep your friends away from here. He doesn't care if they're innocent. He got rid of Rory, didn't he? Well, he can harm your friends, too."

Elizabeth could feel Jessica trembling violently beside her.

"Don't go yet," Nicholas whispered, putting his hand restrainingly on Elizabeth's shoulder as she turned to slip back toward the Jeep. "I've got to talk to her."

"Nicholas—" Elizabeth pleaded.

"All right. You two run down to the Jeep and drive halfway down the road, just so you're away from the house a little. I promise I'll be there in a minute."

"Be careful," Elizabeth warned him.

Nicholas nodded. He was staring at the clearing, the expression in his eyes revealing his torment. He couldn't leave without letting Barbara know he had been there.

But he had to wait until Josine was gone.

"Barbara," he called in a whisper.

Josine, who was halfway across the clearing, spun around suspiciously. "What was that?"

Barbara stared with panic at the spot where Nicholas was standing. "Uh—nothing," she choked out. "Josine, I'm just tying my shoe. I'll be right behind you." Josine continued walking.

Nicholas stepped forward from behind the tree. "I tried to find you. I threw pebbles at your window, but you weren't there," he cried, going over to her and taking her in his arms. "I was so worried about you."

Barbara was trembling all over. "Nicholas, you have to go, right now! Uncle John went out with his friend an hour ago, and they'll be back any second. Please—"

Nicholas gently traced her jaw with his finger, and gazed into her eyes. "I'm going for now. But I'll be back to help you."

"You can't come back," Barbara said. "It's too dangerous."

She pulled away from him, her face wet with tears. "Don't you understand?" she asked, moving across the clearing. "I love you too much to ever let you come back!"

She turned away and ran back toward the house. For a moment Nicholas watched the sheer fabric of her dress shimmer in the moonlight before it disappeared into the woods.

She might as well be a ghost, he thought, his heart breaking. It seemed there was no way he could protect her or rescue her from whatever —or whoever—was threatening her. He loved her with all his heart, but he couldn't seem to take her from her world into his.

Wednesday evening Elizabeth decided to work late. The story on Kincaid wasn't coming together, and she didn't want to admit to Seth that she had been so distracted by Nicholas and Barbara that she hadn't done much research.

By seven-thirty the newsroom was deserted, and Elizabeth found herself working alone in the small, crowded morgue, surrounded by clippings and folders.

She pushed her hair back from her face with a groan and sat down on the floor beside the old black filing cabinets. She still couldn't get Nicholas out of her mind. She knew he had gone back to see Barbara that night, alone. She and Jessica had begged him not to, but Nicholas —an expression of wild determination on his face—had insisted.

Her anxiety wasn't making it any easier to work on this story. She just kept coming up with the same fragments. Kincaid, the art student. Kincaid, the fast-talking businessman. Kincaid and his brother . . . Elizabeth was so frustrated that by eight o'clock she decided to take a break and see if she could find anything new on Paul Lazarow. Maybe she could help Nicholas somehow by learning more about Barbara's grandmother's death. But again she found nothing but the same old stuff: how Lazarow had studied in Paris, then come to Ronoma County to start his artists' colony; how prestigious it was considered to work with him; how his only child had drowned tragically on her twenty-first birthday. After his daughter's death, there seemed to be no trace of him.

As Elizabeth reached into a cabinet to remove the remainder of the Lazarow file, she discovered it was stuck. She leaned over to investigate and found the hanging folder had broken. While she tried to readjust the metal hanger, her fingers brushed a thin, dry piece of paper laying crumpled beneath the broken file. She carefully maneuvered it out of the cabinet so she wouldn't tear it. It was a newspaper article, yellowed with age, with "Lazarow" written across the top to indicate in which folder it should be filed.

Elizabeth scanned the article. The name Russell Kincaid was underlined. Kincaid, she thought, puzzled. What was an article about Kincaid doing in the Lazarow file? She smoothed out the crumpled sheet and began to read. The headline had been cut off, but Kincaid's picture headed the article. It was dated August 1948, and it was the same picture Seth had shown her earlier without any article attached.

Russell Kincaid, twenty-one, was questioned this morning at the Ronoma County Courthouse in Denning, California, at the inquest of the death-by-drowning of Barbara Lazarow, the only child of renowned artist Paul Lazarow. Kincaid denied any involvement in the girl's death. His attorney,

Oliver Patterson, denies reports that Kincaid was seen on the slippery cliffs with Miss Lazarow immediately before her death. No charges have been filed, and the coroner's report confirmed that the victim's death was caused by accidental drowning.

Elizabeth couldn't believe her eyes. Kincaid had been questioned at Barbara Lazarow's inquest? A candidate for mayor had been present—possibly—at the scene of her death?

She stared at the yellowed clipping, a sickening feeling overcoming her. She couldn't believe what she had found. Could that explain the expression of horror on Kincaid's face when he saw Barbara in Denning?

Something else was strange about the article: it didn't mention anything about Barbara Lazarow's husband or her baby. But Nicholas's Barbara was proof that they had existed. What happened to the baby and to Barbara's husband—named Jack, Josine had said—after Barbara died?

Exactly what had taken place at Bayview House? And why did it seem to be starting all over again?

Elizabeth slammed the file drawer shut. Her hands were trembling violently. Russell Kincaid looked so familiar to her, just as he had the first time she had seen his picture in his high school yearbook, as though she knew his gestures, how his voice would sound. Yet she had only seen him, young or old, in photographs, never in person. Where had she seen that face before?

Suddenly she realized. He had the same dark, menacing eyes as Barbara's uncle. Kincaid and Barbara's uncle looked enough alike to be—

"Brothers," she cried out loud. And they even looked about the same age now. "John must be Russell Kincaid's brother!"

Elizabeth spent the next hour feverishly going through the files on Kincaid, trying to find any mention of the brother he had been in business with. At twenty minutes to nine the phone rang.

It was Jessica. "Why aren't you home yet? I was getting worried," she said.

"Hi, Jess," Elizabeth said excitedly. "I'm glad I decided to work late tonight. I think I found out something incredibly important."

"What?"

"Well . . ." Elizabeth hunched over the phone. "I kept having this creepy feeling that I knew Barbara's uncle from somewhere. Tonight I found an incredible story about Kincaid in the file. It looks like he may have been present at the time of Barbara's grandmother's death. And when I was looking at the picture of him, I suddenly realized why Barbara's uncle looked so familiar to me. Jess, he and Russell have almost identical features. Russell's better-looking and a little less heavy, and I would guess he's about five years older. John must be Kincaid's younger brother!"

Jessica was silent for a minute. "And Kincaid was somehow involved in the first Barbara's death. These coincidences are really getting scary, Liz."

"I know. It is pretty remarkable. I've got to let Nicholas know what I found out," Elizabeth said.

Jessica's voice changed suddenly. "Oh, hi, Mom," she called brightly. "Liz, can I call you back? Mom and Dad just walked in."

"Sure," Elizabeth said. "But I'll be home soon. I don't have that much stuff left to do here tonight anyway."

"I'll call you back in two minutes," Jessica said.

No sooner had Elizabeth hung up the phone than it rang again. "Boy, that was quick," she said with a laugh after picking up the receiver. "That was the shortest two minutes in history."

There was no answer. She could hear heavy breathing on the other end of the line.

"Jess, cut it out," she warned. "This isn't funny."

"I'll tell you what isn't funny," a deep, muffled voice said. "What isn't funny is poking into other people's private business. And hanging out where you're not wanted. Am I making myself clear?"

Elizabeth was so frightened, she could barely breathe. "Who is this?" she managed to ask.

"Listen to me, Miss Wakefield," the man snarled. "I know who you are. That's all that matters. I don't particularly care for you to know who I am. Just get this through your pretty little blond head. *We're watching you.* We know exactly where you are. And we don't intend to let you get in our way. Do you understand?"

Elizabeth was trembling all over. She was completely alone in the office. Half the lights had been dimmed when people left hours ago. Was it Barbara's uncle on the phone? What if he was calling from the building? What if he trapped her here?

"I've given you and your friend Mr. Morrow three other warnings," the man went on in a sinister voice. "First I left a message. Then there was the dog. Third, the Jeep. This is it. Remember the old saying—three strikes and you're out. Well, you've had your three strikes—and

137

one more." He laughed—a sinister laugh. "Barbara's birthday is coming up, you know? Maybe you should tell her to be careful. Sometimes birthdays can be unlucky." And before Elizabeth could say a word in protest, he had hung up the phone.

Elizabeth was petrified. She had no idea what to do.

To her absolute horror, the phone rang again.

After seven rings she picked it up. "Uh—hello?" she gasped.

"Liz, where were you?" Jessica demanded crossly. "Didn't I tell you it was only going to be a minute before I called back?"

"Yeah," Elizabeth mumbled. She heard a sound behind her, and she was certain she was going to faint. She fought hard not to scream. "Jess," she said as calmly as she could. "I'm coming home—right away. If I don't get there in fifteen minutes, I want you to call the police."

Ten

On Thursday morning Elizabeth arranged an emergency meeting in the coffee shop that was located downstairs in the *News* building.

"I can't believe he called and threatened you," Nicholas cried, slipping into a seat across from Elizabeth and Jessica.

She glanced fearfully around the room. "What scares me most is that he gave me the impression he was watching every move I made. That's why I didn't call the police. I had the feeling he would find out—and punish Barbara for it. Oh, Nicholas, it was so horrible!"

"I believe you, Liz. I think Barbara must be in terrible danger, and it's all my fault," Nicholas muttered, his hands clenched into fists. "Barbara's birthday is tomorrow. I'm getting her out of there tonight!" He leaned forward, looking from one twin to the other. "I'm going out to Bayview House at about eight-thirty or nine. Just after dark. If you guys come with me . . ."

The twins stared at each other.

"I know it's asking a lot," Nicholas said. "But this time I really need your help. If we're going to kidnap Barbara—"

"How are we going to do that?" Jessica asked.

Nicholas took a deep breath. "One of you will stay in the Jeep with the motor running and the lights out. The other"—he coughed, not meeting either of their gazes—"will distract Barbara's uncle while I help her escape."

"Nicholas," Jessica cried in a low voice, glancing around her to make sure no one was listening, "have you completely lost your mind? That isn't exactly what I'd call a fair division of labor."

"Look, it's going to be dangerous for all of us," Nicholas said, gripping the edge of the table. "If I could think of a *single* alternative, you know I wouldn't ask you to do this."

"Nicholas is right, Jess," Elizabeth said quietly. Her eyes were filled with fear, but her voice was very controlled. "We've got to help Barbara."

"OK," Jessica said. "Then I guess I'll be the one who distracts Barbara's uncle."

"No, that's going to be me," Elizabeth cut in.

"No way, Lizzie. I'm not letting you," Jessica said stubbornly.

"Look," Nicholas interrupted, taking out his wallet to pay the bill, "we'll draw straws if it'd make it easier." He glanced from Elizabeth to Jessica. "Can I count on you both?" he asked.

"Of course you can," Elizabeth said warmly, putting her hand on his arm.

"Sure," Jessica mumbled, her eyes on the table.

"Good." Nicholas pulled some bills out of his wallet. "Then I'll pick you up at seven o'clock." He cleared his throat again. "I want to be sure to reach Bayview House before nightfall."

"You must be totally out of your mind," Jessica cried as she followed her sister into the elevator. "Do you realize what we just agreed to do?"

"What choice do we have?" Elizabeth demanded, pressing the button for their floor. She crossed her arms and leaned back, watching the numbers light up as the elevator rose. "Look, I'm no happier about this than you are, believe me. But we can't exactly desert Nicholas. And he's right, Jess. We can't leave Barbara there alone!"

Jessica sighed heavily. "I don't see why we can't just go to the police."

Elizabeth shook her head. "That may have been the thing to do earlier this week. But at this point, if a policeman shows up to question John, there wouldn't be enough evidence for a charge. And the minute the policeman left, he would probably do something terrible. We can't take that chance, Jess. We've got to do it Nicholas's way."

The elevator doors opened, and the twins walked out onto the fifth-floor *News* offices in silence, both too distraught to speak.

They hadn't gotten very far when Dan Weeks stopped them.

"Jessica, how are you coming along with your work on the Lazarow story?" he asked. He had a manila folder in his hands.

Jessica glanced at her sister. "I think I'm on to something, Dan. But it looks like the story is much bigger than I thought at first."

Dan nodded seriously. "You mean you've found out that the Lazarow story seems to link up somehow with the Kincaid story?"

Elizabeth's eyes widened. "You mean you've found that out, too? But do you know how they link up?" she asked eagerly.

Dan shook his head. "Not yet. Mr. Robb just

gave me this folder of material, which was apparently cataloged under the name of Lazarow's colony." He glanced at his watch. "But I have to cover another story this morning and won't have time to look at this for a while. Jessica, would you mind combing through it and taking notes for me on anything you think would be relevant?"

"I'd be happy to," Jessica said, taking the folder from him.

"Jessica, let's go to the newsroom library, where we can shut the door," Elizabeth whispered, the minute Dan was out of earshot. She could barely wait to see what was in that file.

Maybe, just maybe, they would be able to figure out who had killed Barbara Lazarow, and why!

"Let's see," Jessica muttered, pulling the first clipping out of the file. " 'Artist Starts Colony in Ronoma,' " she read. " 'June 1939. California native Paul Lazarow is currently raising money to fund an artists' colony in his hometown.' "

"We knew that already," Elizabeth murmured, reading over her sister's shoulder. "Hey, look at this article," she added.

"Rivalry for Prize Develops Among Art Students," the next headline ran. It was dated July 1947. The article began by describing the colony. " 'A prize is given at the end of the summer to the student showing the most promise,' " Elizabeth read aloud. " 'According to the teachers we interviewed, the top contestants for the prize this summer are Jack Pearsall and Russell Kincaid.' "

"Kincaid!" Elizabeth cried.

"Jack Pearsall," Jessica murmured. "Why . . ." Then her brow cleared. "Isn't *Jack* the name Josine kept asking Barbara about that night we were there?"

"Yes!" Elizabeth exclaimed. "Barbara's husband. But not a single article I've read has even mentioned him or a baby."

Jessica shook her head as she picked up the last of the articles. " 'Behind the Scenes at Bayview House,' " she read aloud. It was a feature story on the artist and his daughter, written late in the spring of 1948, just months before Barbara's death.

Most of the story seemed to repeat information that the twins already knew.

"Wait," Jessica said eagerly, scanning the story. "Listen to this: 'When asked about the rivalry between Jack Pearsall and Russell Kincaid, Barbara Lazarow said only, "They're both good artists. Naturally there's competition." When our reporters wondered about rumors that the two young men were competing for her affection as well, she ended the interview.' "

Elizabeth stared at her. "Let me see that," she said. She picked up the article and stared at it incredulously. "You think Kincaid and this guy Jack were fighting over her?"

"It sure sounds like it," Jessica said.

"But I wonder. . . ." Elizabeth mused. "She was married, wasn't she? And she had a baby girl—Barbara's mother. It doesn't add up." She shook her head. "It's mystifying. But one thing is pretty clear: Kincaid was involved in this whole mystery, somehow, and it's clear he's done an awful lot to cover it up for forty years. Now that he's got such a good shot at winning the race for mayor, he must be all the more uneasy about his past."

"Which means what?" Jessica demanded.

"Look," Elizabeth said seriously, "remember I told you I thought Barbara's uncle looked a lot like Russell Kincaid?"

Jessica nodded.

Elizabeth tapped her fingers on the file. "Why would Kincaid's brother be tormenting Barbara? And what's his connection to Bayview House in the first place?"

"You've got me," Jessica said. "All I know is

that I want to get Barbara out of there and then forget the whole thing ever happened."

Elizabeth didn't respond. She was trying to put together the pieces of the puzzle. But none of them fell into place. All she knew was that Barbara was in terrible danger and they had to get out to Ronoma in time to save Barbara from reliving the *next* chapter of her grandmother's tragic story!

"Do both of you remember exactly what's going to happen?" Nicholas asked as they headed out to Ronoma in his Jeep.

"Who could forget?" Jessica asked grimly.

"We've all got to do our best to stay calm no matter what," Nicholas said. His own expression was anything but calm, though. He was clenching the steering wheel hard, and his knuckles were white from the tension. All three of them had put on dark pants and shirts so they would be less visible.

It seemed to take forever to get to Ronoma. But at last they pulled up the familiar road leading to the gates of Bayview House.

"Look," Jessica cried, grabbing her sister's arm and pointing ahead of them.

There, parked on the shoulder of the road, was the silver-blue Jaguar.

"Well, it looks like we're going to have company. Kincaid's here," Nicholas said grimly, turning off the headlights and cutting the motor of the Jeep.

Jessica was trembling violently. "Nicholas, I want Elizabeth to stay here in the car. I'm going to be the one to distract John."

"Let me just tell you the plan first," Nicholas said. He looked up at the house and frowned. "It's really foggy up there. It may be hard to see. I'm going to run up behind the house and try to get Barbara's attention by throwing pebbles at her window. I want one of you to stay back here. The other one should go up to the house and ring the door bell. Whoever answers, just distract them. If it's Josine, keep her talking while I sneak Barbara out back through the woods. If it's John—"

"Then what?" Jessica demanded nervously.

"You'll have to use your head. And your leg muscles," Nicholas said. "Tell him you've come out to apologize for interfering. Tell him anything you can think of. And if he chases you, run like crazy back to the Jeep."

"Jess, I'm not letting you go. You're staying right here," Elizabeth said firmly.

Nicholas pulled two toothpicks from his pocket. "I brought these. Each of you pick one. Who-

147

ever gets the shorter one will go. The other will stay here in the driver's seat. OK?"

The twins nodded and silently drew their lots.

Elizabeth had the shorter of the two. "Well," she said, taking a deep breath, "that settles that!"

"Come on," Nicholas said. "Liz, are you ready?"

Elizabeth nodded. She couldn't look her sister in the eye, but she knew how Jessica was feeling. Finally she managed to touch her arm. "Take it easy," she whispered.

Jessica's eyes were filling with tears. All she could do was nod to show Elizabeth she had heard her.

The thought of letting her twin deliberately ring that door bell was almost more than Jessica could bear. It was like allowing Elizabeth to walk into a terrible trap. How could she possibly just sit in the Jeep, knowing what kind of danger her twin could be in?

Eleven

The fog was thickening as Nicholas and Elizabeth slipped around to the side of the Jeep and darted across the road to the trail leading up through the woods. The gravel was slippery from the moisture, and twice Elizabeth almost stumbled.

"Wait a sec," Nicholas said with a gasp, slowing down. He was out of breath, and so was Elizabeth. "Do you hear that?"

Elizabeth was quiet, straining to hear over the distant waves. "No," she said at last. "Hear what?"

"Someone behind us," Nicholas said. "I could've sworn I heard footsteps." He started hurrying up the trail again.

Elizabeth could barely see two feet in front of

her. It was very dark in the woods and impossible for Elizabeth to keep up with Nicholas without falling on the slippery forest floor. "Nicholas," she called softly. "Can you slow down a little?" But Nicholas didn't seem to hear her.

"Nicholas, wait," Elizabeth cried. Her hands were sweating, and she slipped again, catching herself just in time by grabbing onto a tree. Nicholas continued to charge up the trail toward the house.

Elizabeth regained her balance and started to run after him. Then her left foot caught on a root, and she fell forward, hard. An excruciating pain shot through her leg, and she cried out involuntarily. She couldn't move at all.

The fog was so thick, she couldn't see Nicholas anywhere on the path. She called out his name.

"I'm up here!" he called back. "Come on."

"I can't!" she cried back. "I hurt myself!"

"Liz!" a frightened voice cried. Elizabeth saw Jessica rushing toward her. "Liz, I just couldn't stand staying in that Jeep alone, thinking about you out here. And I kept hearing these awful creaks and weird noises," she said, tears running down her face.

"Oh, Jess, thank God," Elizabeth cried. "I think I sprained my ankle. Nicholas is already up at the house. He doesn't know I fell. You'd better run up ahead. Ring the bell, distract Josine or John or whoever answers." She winced as she tried to get up. "Are the keys still in the Jeep? I'll crawl back there and stay with the car."

Jessica's eyes were wide with terror. "You want me to go up to the house?" she shrieked. "How can I leave you here if you're hurt?"

"We can't leave Nicholas up there alone. Go on, Jess," Elizabeth urged. "Don't worry. I'll make it."

Jessica sighed. "All right. But if anything happens, lean on the horn, OK? I'll come back to you as fast as I can."

Elizabeth nodded and gave her twin a little push. "Go on. Help him." And the next minute her twin was gone, darting through the dark woods to the house.

Elizabeth looked down at her rapidly swelling ankle. "This is just great," she muttered, grabbing hold of the tree next to her and trying to pull herself up. "Talk about terrific timing. Now all I need is for—"

Out of nowhere a flashlight beam bounced across the clearing and settled right on Elizabeth. A deep, sinister voice cried out, "Don't move!"

Elizabeth's mouth dropped open as she got to her feet. The light was so bright, she had to look away. But she recognized the voice.

It was John.

"Now I've got you," he snarled, inching forward. His face was set in a horrible scowl, but the only thing Elizabeth really noticed was the silver revolver in his hand, pointing directly at her. "You thought you'd play heroine, right? By barging onto someone else's property and butting in where you don't belong. Was that the idea?"

Elizabeth couldn't speak. Not a sound came out. She just stared at the silver gun, her heart beating so rapidly, she was sure it would explode.

"Well, you can forget about all that now," the man cried. He crossed the clearing in a few long strides and grabbed her roughly by the arm, yanking her toward him. Pain shot through her ankle, and she cried out.

"Shut up!" John shouted, striking her hard.

Elizabeth drew back in horror from the blow. Her eyes filled with tears from the stinging pain, but her voice, when she spoke, was perfectly controlled. "Why are you doing this?" she demanded. "What do you want with Barbara?"

"That's none of your business," the man

snapped, shaking her roughly. "Forget the stupid questions. You're coming with me now." He glowered unpleasantly.

"You're Russell Kincaid's brother, aren't you?" Elizabeth asked.

Her words had exactly the effect she had hoped they would. The man stepped back, his expression startled. "How did you figure that out?" he demanded. "It doesn't matter who I am, especially not to you." He started to drag Elizabeth with him up the trail, twisting her arm roughly behind her.

"Just tell me why you're doing this," Elizabeth choked out.

"That louse cheated me out of a million dollars when he broke our partnership," he muttered. "And I wanted to expose him for something he did forty years ago. I knew they'd never elect a murderer for mayor. I had to expose him in a very subtle way, or he would have had me killed." He pushed Elizabeth forward, ignoring her cries. "So I decided to convince him that his old girlfriend Barbara had come back from the grave to haunt him. It was easy," he mumbled. "At least, it was easy until you three started getting in my way. All I had to do was invite the granddaughter here for the summer and force her to play ghost."

Elizabeth felt a wave of cold horror wash over her. So Russell Kincaid really *had* murdered Barbara Lazarow!

"Where are you taking me?" she cried, trying to pull away from his steely grasp. "Let me go!" she shouted, struggling harder.

"Listen to me," John Kincaid snarled, twisting her arm hard. "Either you come with me without a struggle, or I'll make it easy for you.

"Here's a little guarantee that you won't be asking any more questions." He jabbed the revolver in her side, and Elizabeth gasped at the pressure of the cold metal. She twisted around as far as she could and tried to kick him with her injured foot.

"That's it, you little idiot," he cried. He lifted the revolver, blunt end forward, and swung it at Elizabeth's temple. She screamed out in pain. Then there was only darkness.

"Nicholas, where are you?" Jessica called out. "I banged and banged on the front door. No one answered!" She was running along the cliff trail behind the house, trying to find Nicholas.

"I'm here!" Nicholas cried, less than ten feet in front of her. He pointed in the distance, to a place where a shadowy figure was visible in the mist. "I'm going after them!" He took off at a furious pace.

Jessica nodded and started to run after him. Then she saw him stop short.

"Stop!" he screamed at the top of his lungs. "Stop it!"

Jessica tried to see what was happening. It was so foggy, it was almost impossible to see. Nicholas was shouting Barbara's name. The whole world seemed to reverberate with the echo of his terrible cry. Then the fog momentarily lifted, and Jessica saw two shadowy figures struggling on the edge of the cliff. One was a heavy-set, dark-haired man. The other was Barbara.

"Nicholas!" Jessica cried, watching the scene before her in horror. But Nicholas was already stumbling over the trail, racing toward Barbara.

"Barbara, hang on! I'm coming!" he called out as he scrambled toward her across the steep cliff. Below them the tide was pounding fiercely against the jagged rocks.

Jessica covered her face with her hands. The man was trying to push Barbara over the edge of the cliff and into the sea.

She lifted her hands again and realized the man was Russell Kincaid. He had grasped Barbara around both wrists and was pulling her with all his might. The next instant he slipped and fell backward, pulling Barbara with him.

"Barbara!" Nicholas screamed.

His voice echoed for a moment. Then Jessica heard nothing but the crashing waves, followed by another cry from Nicholas. "Liz! Come help me!"

It took Jessica an instant to realize that Nicholas thought she was Elizabeth. She stumbled toward him, shaking all over, terrified of what they would find on the other side of the cliffs. Nicholas was on his knees, stretching out toward the first ledge of the rocks.

And there was Barbara, hanging on to a narrow ledge beneath him! She had miraculously managed to catch herself there. Below her the wild surf pounded over the rocks where Kincaid must have fallen.

"Barbara!" Nicholas screamed over the sound of the waves. "Don't let go! I'm coming to get you. Hang on!"

He turned back to Jessica with a look of anguish. "She's losing her grip. I've got to jump down and get her." Before Jessica could respond, Nicholas was crawling down onto the slippery ledge. He was halfway across when one of Barbara's hands gave way, and she screamed.

156

"I've got you. I've got you," Nicholas sobbed as he dragged Barbara over the ledge. He wrapped her in his arms and held her until they both stopped trembling. Then he lifted her up, and Jessica grabbed Barbara's hands and helped pull her up to the spot where she herself was standing. Nicholas pulled himself up and stood.

"Are you all right?" Nicholas asked Barbara, tenderly brushing the damp hair back from her face.

"I—I think so," she stammered. She was white as a sheet. "Where's Uncle John?" She shook her head, struggling to speak. "He tied up Josine inside. He has a gun," she said weakly. "We have to get help."

"A gun!" Jessica cried, jumping to her feet. "You guys, we have to go back and find Liz. She hurt her ankle. When I left her, she was trying to get back to the Jeep. But if she couldn't make it . . ."

"Liz?" Nicholas repeated incredulously. Then, in recognition, he cried, "Jessica! But I thought—"

"I'll explain later. Just help me now," Jessica gasped.

She began to run back to the place in the woods where she had last seen her sister. The whole time she berated herself for leaving Elizabeth hurt and alone. "I should've stayed with her," she kept crying.

"Where was she? Here?" Nicholas demanded, staring wildly around him.

"Maybe she's in the Jeep," Jessica cried disconsolately.

But the Jeep was empty, and Elizabeth was nowhere to be seen.

"Wait," Barbara cried, scooping down and picking up a gold chain that had caught on a root. "What's this?"

At that point Jessica began to sob in earnest. It was her twin's lavaliere necklace. Each had been given one when she turned sixteen, and neither twin ever took hers off.

"We've got to find her," Jessica cried, grabbing Nicholas by the arm.

Barbara was staring down at the lavaliere, her face completely white. She looked as though she might faint.

"I think she's in shock," Nicholas cried, jumping forward to catch her.

Barbara shook her head, fighting for control. "No," she said weakly. "I'm OK." She stared at him, her eyes filling with tears. "It was just . . . when I saw the necklace, I thought of poor Rory. And then I remembered the look on that man's face as he fell over into the sea."

158

Twelve

"It's all my fault," Jessica sobbed as they ran toward the house. "I should never have left her there. It was just—she told me to run up and ring the door bell—I was afraid everything would be ruined otherwise. . . ." She tried to control herself, but she couldn't stop shaking.

"We'll find her, Jess," Nicholas said, trying to comfort her. "Don't panic."

"The best thing we can do is find Josine," Barbara said. "She'll be able to help us. She'll know where Uncle John has taken Liz."

"What if she's—" Jessica's eyes were wide with terror.

"Jess, she'll be OK," Nicholas assured her. But he was frightened, too. "I should never have let you two come out here," he mumbled, hurrying up to the house and trying the front door.

"It's locked. Let's go around back," Barbara urged, running around the side of the house.

The house was completely dark inside. "Darn it," Barbara said, trying a switch as the others entered the house behind her. "He cut the power!"

Jessica shivered with fear.

"Well, we'll just have to grope our way to the kitchen," Barbara said. "Follow me, you guys." They were standing in an entryway.

"Hurry," Jessica moaned. She couldn't stand not knowing where Elizabeth was.

"Josine," Barbara called softly as she crept into the kitchen. They heard a moan, and in the dim moonlight coming through the kitchen window they saw Josine, tied to a chair, her mouth gagged with a dish towel.

"Oh, no!" Barbara moaned as she ran to her.

Josine started crying as Barbara and Nicholas hastened to untie her. "I thought he got you," she said to Barbara.

Barbara threw her arms around the old house-keeper as soon as she was free. "I'm fine," she whispered emotionally. She didn't tell Josine what had happened to Kincaid. Jessica waited silently for Barbara to ask about Elizabeth.

"Where's Uncle John?" Barbara demanded urgently.

This only made Josine cry harder. "I don't know. He had a gun. He tied me up, threatened me, called me an old idiot." She lifted her tear-stained face. "I thought it was happening all over again." She shook her head. "I warned you it would never work! Whoever heard of keeping a marriage a secret from your own father? And me! If you'd told me, I could've helped you. But when the baby came, you couldn't hide it anymore, could you? I knew all along what Russell would do. He loved you so much, he couldn't bear letting anyone else have you. Not Jack . . ."

"Josine, it's me. Not my grandmother," Barbara said, kneeling down and looking pleadingly into her eyes. "Remember? I'm Barbara's granddaughter."

Josine stared at her as if in a daze. "But what happened to the baby?" she asked pitifully. "Jack wanted to find her!" She sighed sadly, wiping her face and looking around her as if she were trying to determine where she was.

Nicholas put his hand on Barbara's shoulder. "Barbara," he said in a low voice, "I think we'd better try to find Liz. Do you think Josine can help us?"

Barbara looked anxiously at him. "Let me try," she said softly.

She turned back to the old woman and said, very gently, "Josine, we're in trouble. We think Uncle John may be trying to hurt our friend. We need to find him."

Suddenly Josine seemed to be wrenched back to the present. She trembled all over, and her expression was one of pure terror. "He has a gun!" she cried.

"Where is he?" Barbara asked.

Josine's eyes flashed. "He isn't your uncle, you know," she said furiously. "He's Russell Kincaid's brother, and I would've told you so the minute you got here if he hadn't threatened to kill me." She buried her face in her hands. "I get confused sometimes. . . . I'm so old. He knew that, he took advantage." She stared sorrowfully at Barbara. "He only brought you here this summer so he could drive his brother mad. I was trapped. There was nothing I could do to help."

Jessica didn't think she could bear it a minute longer. "Josine," she interrupted. "We think Barbara's uncle—or Kincaid's brother or whoever he is—is trying to hurt my sister. If we don't find her right away . . ."

Josine stared at Jessica, her eyes wide with

fear. "What are you doing here?" she cried. "I thought he knocked you out!" She looked desperately at Barbara. "He came in here carrying a girl—I thought it was her—she had blond hair . . ."

Jessica felt as if she were going to pass out. "Carrying her?" she echoed weakly.

Josine nodded. "She wasn't moving. He told me to sit still and shut up or soon I wouldn't be moving either."

Jessica grabbed hold of Nicholas's arm. She was too horrified to scream.

"Josine," Barbara cried, "what did he do with her? Where was he going?"

"He—he took her back outside. He got the key for the studio and left."

"Let's go," Nicholas said. And before anyone else could say or do a thing, Nicholas was tearing out the back door.

Nicholas reached the studio before Jessica and Barbara. It was a small octagonal stone building with a wooden door and high windows, built for total privacy.

"It's locked," Nicholas cried, yanking on the door.

"We *have* to get in," Jessica moaned, pulling uselessly at the doorknob after Nicholas let go.

Barbara backed up, eyeing the uppermost win-

163

dow. It was open. "Nicholas, do you think you can give me a boost? I should just be able to reach the window."

Nicholas bent down and helped Barbara to step onto his shoulders. With agonizing precision he stood up, as slowly as he could, and approached the window.

A minute later they heard a soft thud as Barbara jumped down into the studio. It only took a minute for her to unlock the door, but that minute felt like centuries to Jessica.

The first thing she was aware of when Barbara flung open the door was the sound of barking. Rory was running around them in frantic circles, intoxicated with joy at finding his mistress again.

"Rory!" Barbara cried, scooping up her precious dog and covering him with kisses. She stepped farther into the studio and spotted Elizabeth lying on the floor. "Hurry," she urged Nicholas and Jessica. "Elizabeth is over here. It looks as if she's badly hurt."

"Liz!" Jessica cried, dropping down on her knees and studying her sister's expressionless face.

"Jess, be careful," Nicholas said. "She might be in shock." He shucked off his sweater and used it to cover Elizabeth.

"Barbara, can I use your sweater as a pillow?" he asked. Barbara handed it to him wordlessly, and Nicholas gently slipped it beneath Elizabeth's head.

"Oh, Lizzie," Jessica moaned, stroking her sister's face. "Please, please wake up!"

"We have to call an ambulance," Barbara said softly. "I'll run back to the house and call."

Nicholas frowned. "Where's John?"

Barbara shivered. "Probably far from here by now! He thinks he's done everything he needed to. As far as he knows, I'm in the same place that his brother is."

"Well, I'd feel better making the call myself," Nicholas said. "You stay here with Jessica."

Barbara nodded assent, and the two girls watched him stride off.

"Do you think she's going to be all right?" Jessica asked softly, picking up her sister's limp hand and squeezing it tightly. Not a single flicker of awareness crossed Elizabeth's face.

"Let's hope so," Barbara whispered. "If anything happened to her, I'd never forgive myself for as long as I live."

Rory, still ecstatic to have been found, jumped out of Barbara's arms and began licking Elizabeth's face. "Rory, stop it," Barbara scolded, scooping him back into her arms.

Suddenly Elizabeth groaned and moved her head from side to side.

"Liz!" Jessica shrieked.

"Don't try to talk," Barbara said quickly, putting her hand gently against Elizabeth's face. "We're here, Liz. We've called an ambulance. You're going to be fine."

"My head . . ." Elizabeth moaned. "What happened?"

"Liz, don't even think or talk or anything," Jessica cried, thrilled that her sister was conscious. "Just lie still. Nicholas has gone to call an ambulance. We're going to get you out of here any second."

Elizabeth seemed to be fighting for control. "I should never have tried to struggle," she whispered drowsily. "When I saw the gun, I should've just gone with him."

"It was John Kincaid, wasn't it?" Jessica asked, shuddering. "Liz, when I think that I left you lying there with that sprained ankle, knowing he was somewhere nearby—how can you ever forgive me?"

Barbara shook her head. "I'm the one who needs to be forgiven. If it weren't for me, neither of you would've been in this situation in the first place!"

Elizabeth pressed her sister's hand. "Are you

OK, both of you?" she whispered weakly. "Barbara, you're safe?"

Barbara nodded. She had to lean forward and nuzzle Rory's neck to hide her emotion. "You three saved my life," she said emotionally. "I don't even know what to say to you." She cleared her throat. "Nicholas, well, Nicholas loves me. I know that. But you two—you came out here and risked your lives for me. You don't even know me! I feel—" She broke off, unable to go on.

"I'm so glad you're both safe," Elizabeth murmured, her eyes still closed.

"You're the one we're worried about!" Jessica cried fearfully.

Elizabeth opened her eyes and looked directly into her twin's. "I'm OK," she whispered. "It's just my head—it hurts so much!"

Jessica and Barbara exchanged anguished glances. It seemed to take forever before Nicholas came back, and even longer before the ambulance arrived and the emergency medics ran up from the road with a stretcher.

Jessica stared disconsolately at her sister's face as she was lifted onto the stretcher. "Please take care of her," she whispered to the medics.

"You know," one of the medics said, winking, "you look so much like her, we might have to let you ride with us in the ambulance. How does that sound?"

Jessica looked tearfully at Nicholas and Barbara. "Would that be all right? Will you guys meet me at the hospital?"

"We'll try. We've got to check on Josine. I called the police. They should be here any minute, but I don't know how long they'll take. Once I know what's happening, I'll call the hospital."

They all walked behind the medics out to the road, and Jessica climbed into the ambulance and sat down next to Elizabeth.

Nicholas and Barbara stood still for a minute, watching the red bubble light of the ambulance spinning around and around. Barbara was pale.

"I hope she's all right," she whispered.

Nicholas squeezed her hand tightly. "Me, too," he whispered back.

Not until the ambulance had pulled away, its siren blaring, did Nicholas realize why the road looked different. His Jeep was still parked in the same place. But Russell Kincaid's Jaguar was gone.

Thirteen

"Can someone around here please explain to me what's going on?" Ned Wakefield demanded, bursting into the emergency room of Joshua Fowler Memorial Hospital.

"Daddy!" Jessica cried, throwing her arms around her father and bursting into tears.

Alice Wakefield raced in right behind her husband. "Where's Liz? Is she all right?" she cried.

"I'll explain in a minute," Jessica promised, wiping her eyes. "The doctor said he'd be out any second to tell us how Liz is."

Jessica had called her parents soon after she got to the hospital. For the past half hour she had been waiting in total agony while Dr. Fisherman, a resident working the emergency room that night, ran some tests to make sure Elizabeth hadn't suffered serious injuries. "It was so horrible," Jessica said, shuddering. "We were trying to help Nicholas's friend Barbara, and there was this awful man who was trying to kill her—or not kill her, but—"

Mr. Wakefield interrupted her garbled explanation. "I think the doctor's coming."

Dr. Fisherman entered the waiting room. "You must be the Wakefields," he said, looking up from his clipboard and smiling. "Elizabeth is being x-rayed at the moment. I'll have a neurologist look at her, but from the preliminary tests, it appears that she is going to be just fine."

Jessica let out a cry of joy.

"Thank heavens," Mrs. Wakefield said under her breath, then sank back into a chair, visibly relieved.

"She's a very lucky young woman. The blow she received to the head was quite strong. If it had been an inch or two lower"—Dr. Fisherman shook his head—"she could have suffered very serious damage. But it appears she's only received a mild concussion. We'll know more, of course, after we've seen the X rays. We'll also x-ray her ankle, although it just seems to be sprained. I'd like to keep her here overnight. If she doesn't have a skull fracture, I don't see why we can't send her home first thing tomorrow morning. Otherwise, we'll keep her under observation for a day or two."

"Can we see her?" Jessica asked.

Dr. Fisherman smiled. "You certainly can. She's been asking about you. I'm afraid you'll have to wait for a while, however. After she's finished with her X rays, I want to admit her directly to a room. Then you'll be able to see her." He shook Mr. Wakefield's hand. "From the story I've been hearing from your daughter, I think you have two very brave girls here, sir."

"We haven't heard a thing yet," Mr. Wakefield said, clearing his throat. "But now that the panic's over, maybe someone"—he looked meaningfully at Jessica—"could explain what happened tonight."

"Let's wait until we see Liz first," Jessica begged. "Then we can tell you together."

An hour later the twins had filled their parents in on most of the details about their terrifying evening at Bayview House.

"The last thing I knew, you were heading back to the Jeep," Jessica said to Elizabeth. "When we came back, and we found your necklace on the ground—"

"My necklace!" Elizabeth exclaimed, reaching up to her throat. "Where is it? It must've fallen off when John Kincaid grabbed me!"

"I've got it," Jessica assured her. "But I have to tell you, I practically fainted. Knowing that man had a gun, that you were injured and he must've dragged you off somewhere . . ."

"It makes me positively sick to think of you girls being chased by this criminal," Mrs. Wakefield cried. "Where is he now? Have the police been notified?"

"Nicholas and Barbara were waiting for them when the ambulance came," Jessica replied. "I hope they can catch him," she added. "For all we know, he could be over the border already."

"Let's turn on the news," Elizabeth said, reaching for the remote control and turning on the TV at the end of the bed.

The late-night news was almost over, but the newscaster paused to review the story that had just come over the wires. "Again, we repeat the lead story: Russell Kincaid, the mayoral candidate, has been discovered drowned tonight off the coast of Ronoma. Police have not yet determined how the accident occurred, but investigations are under way. Russell Kincaid, candidate for mayor, dead tonight at the age of sixty-one. We'll have an update as soon as we have more information."

"I can't believe it," Elizabeth whispered, shaking her head. "We were all trying so hard to find out who he really was and what kind of dark secret he was hiding. Now we'll never know for sure!"

"That isn't true," Jessica said. "If the police find John Kincaid, the story will all come together. I just know it will, Liz."

Elizabeth hoped her sister was right.

When the news was over, Mr. and Mrs. Wakefield and Jessica stood up to go just as the phone rang.

"Who can that be?" Mr. Wakefield asked.

"It's Nicholas," Elizabeth said after she answered. "I'm fine. What about you? And Barbara?"

A minute later she covered the receiver with her hand. "Nicholas is at the police station with Barbara, Jess. He wants you to meet him there."

Mr. Wakefield frowned at his watch. "Can't it wait till tomorrow? It's awfully late."

"Can Jessica come in the morning?" Elizabeth asked Nicholas.

"Forget it, Liz. I don't mind going now," Jessica said. "You guys can drop me off there on your way home, and Nicholas can bring me home when we're done." She shrugged. "I won't be able to sleep now anyway. I'm so keyed up after everything that's happened."

Mrs. Wakefield sighed. "I guess we don't have much choice. If they're trying to find this horrible man, you'll have to help them, Jess. But don't let them keep you too long."

Jessica nodded impatiently. She could hardly wait to get to the police station to find out what was going on.

The scene that greeted her when her parents dropped her off ten minutes later was fairly subdued. The station was very quiet. One officer was sitting behind a desk, reading through some papers, and Barbara and Nicholas were back in an office with a police detective.

Detective Clark was a short, pleasant-looking man with a firm handshake. He was taking furious notes as Barbara explained her version of the story.

"Until I came to Ronoma this summer," Barbara began, "I didn't know very much about my grandmother—my mother's mother. My mother also knew very little. When I received an invitation to spend the summer here, it seemed like a perfect opportunity for me to learn more." She explained that her parents were away in Greece for the summer, doing research. "The letter inviting me came from a man claiming to be my grandmother's cousin. He called himself Uncle John."

"John Kincaid," the detective said, scribbling furiously.

Barbara nodded. "Yes, I guess so. But I didn't know a thing about Kincaid. He told us his name was John Blake. He even came to Switzerland and met my parents. He seemed perfectly nice then. But the moment I arrived here, he acted like a completely different man. He treated me very strangely. He asked me to wear my grandmother's clothing, suggested—insisted, really—that I take walks up on the cliffs at dusk, on the nights when this visitor—his brother, I guess—would come. Not every night but some nights. Other times he made me go to my room. I was never allowed to see this man."

"Russell Kincaid," Detective Clark added.

"I tried asking him why he made me do this stuff, but he'd get furious, start screaming, tell me he'd do all sorts of horrible things to Josine—the housekeeper—if I didn't obey. He never threatened me directly until this week."

The detective nodded. "And when did you meet these others, Nicholas and the Wakefield twins?"

Barbara told him about the picnic and how Elizabeth and Nicholas had accidentally wandered onto the property. "By that point I knew something frightening was going on, but I wasn't

175

sure what it was. I was very scared of Uncle John—I mean, *Mr.* Kincaid—and so pleased to meet people my own age. I thought that perhaps they could help me—maybe go to the police and tell someone I was in trouble. But—" She broke off and fiddled with her bracelet. "I liked them all so much, and I realized at once that if they interfered, their lives would be in jeopardy. I knew this man I thought then was a relative was dangerous and would harm anyone who stood in the way of his plans."

"And what was your understanding of those plans?" the police detective asked.

Barbara cleared her throat. "I was never completely sure. But I knew it had something to do with the visitor—the man who turned out to be his brother. I think John Kincaid wanted his brother to see me up on the cliffs and think I was my grandmother. But I'm not exactly sure why. I just know that I was important to his plan, so he didn't want anything to happen to me."

Detective Clark asked Nicholas and Jessica a number of questions before thanking them and telling them they could go home and get some sleep.

"Sir," Barbara asked nervously, "do you have any lead on where Mr. Kincaid is?"

The detective was about to answer when a loud commotion came from the front of the station. Doors burst open, lights snapped on, and two officers came hurrying in, dragging the handcuffed, furious John Kincaid between them. "We found him heading for Mexico!" one of the officers cried.

John Kincaid glowered at the floor, not meeting the gazes of anyone in the room. Detective Clark got up and crossed the room to look him in the face. "Well, Mr. Kincaid, it looks like we've got you," he said. "Anytime you feel like cooperating and telling us a little bit about what's happened tonight, we'd be more than willing to listen."

It seemed like ages before John Kincaid lifted his head and began his confession. He didn't seem to care when the policeman read him his rights and reminded him he could call his lawyer before saying anything.

"I don't have a lawyer," he muttered. "It's all over for me, anyway." He glared at Nicholas and Jessica. "If it weren't for you, it would've gone the way I planned it. Down to the last detail. I had it all worked out so perfectly. I was never going to hurt her," he added, jerking his

177

head at Barbara. "Russell was the one I wanted to get. And Russell had it coming to him."

"Why don't you explain to us what happened," Detective Clark said calmly.

Jessica couldn't get over how broken-down and exhausted the man looked. Much of the fierceness was gone from his eyes, and he didn't look half as frightening as he had the last time she had seen him. It was as if the violence in him had been fueled only as long as his brother was alive. Now that Russell was dead, John Kincaid just looked sad and weary.

Detective Clark motioned for one of the officers to start the tape recorder. "Go on," he prodded.

John shifted his weight. "The real story started a long, long time ago. More than forty years. This girl"—he gestured at Barbara—"had a grandmother, also named Barbara. A very beautiful girl. She was too old for me, though. I was just a kid. Russ was the one in love with her." He sighed, thinking back. "And love wasn't the word for what my older brother felt. He was obsessed with her. He met her when he was a student—an art student—studying with her father. Barbara's father was a well-known painter, and my brother had fantasies then of becoming famous himself, marrying Barbara, living happily ever after in Ronoma." He coughed bitterly. "But he was a fool. He didn't know it, but Barbara was in love with another student—Russell's archrival, a young painter named Jack Pearsall. I tried to tell him, but—" He shook his head. "I can't tell you how mad about Barbara my brother was. And *mad* is truly the right word. He wouldn't listen to reason. He used to say if he couldn't have her, no one would. Watching her with Jack made him so sick, he couldn't eat for days. Even though I was young, I tried to talk some sense into him. . . ." He sighed and ran his hands through his hair.

"It wasn't any use. Most of us knew what was going on between Barbara and Jack. I think the only two who didn't know were Russell and Barbara's father. Josine—the Lazarows' housekeeper—used to act as go-between for them. You see, Barbara's father was very protective of her. His wife died shortly after Barbara was born, and he had raised her all alone. So Barbara and Jack ran off together and got married in secret. Soon she had a baby girl.

"Well, Russell was mad with jealousy. Absolutely mad. He managed to get Barbara to meet him up on the cliffs, said he had to see her." John shivered. "It was the night of her birthday. And he killed her. He pushed her over the edge. Later he tried to tell me he was only trying to kiss her and she struggled and slipped and fell. But he couldn't keep it inside. He had to tell someone. We were very close. And he confessed to me that he had pushed her. He said he would rather she was dead than to have to live with the fact that she had loved and married another man."

Everyone in the office was listening raptly as John went on.

"So Russell left Ronoma, and when I turned eighteen, I joined him. We started a business together. We forgot the past. We made a lot of money. I was the brains behind the business. Everything was fine for years." John's eyes filled with tears. "He was my brother. I wanted to protect him. I don't know why he had to do what he did to me."

"What did he do?" the detective prompted him.

"Out of the blue he got this idea that he was going to run for mayor. I couldn't talk him out of it. I told him Sweet Valley was too close to Ronoma, that people might remember what had happened to Barbara. After all, he had testified at her inquest. If Barbara's father hadn't gotten sick right after she died, Russell might even have been convicted.

180

"But Russell wouldn't listen to reason. He had missed out on fame when he gave up his career as an artist, and now he was hungry for it. He had bigger dreams, from mayor to governor, who knows? He wanted his name to be known. And when I wouldn't back him, told him it was a foolish idea, he dissolved our partnership and swindled me out of most of the money I'd earned him—millions of dollars."

Jessica's eyes widened. So that was why John had wanted to get back at his brother!

"I couldn't stand it," John said bitterly. "I'd tried to talk him out of it, and it hadn't worked. So I decided I'd keep him from running any way I could. And I swore to get back at him for what he did to me." He stared at Barbara. "That's when I came up with this brilliant idea."

"What was that?" the detective pressed him.

"Well, I remembered that Barbara's daughter had been raised in Europe by a friend. I went to see Josine, who was very old by now, to ask her if she knew where the daughter was today. It turned out she had gotten a letter from her last Christmas saying she had a girl of her own, named Barbara. There was a photograph in the Christmas card. The girl looked exactly like her grandmother. My plan was simple: invite the girl to spend the summer and pretend to be her grandmother's cousin. Meanwhile, I told my brother I was writing a book on the history of Bayview House and I thought the place was haunted. I got him to come out to the house to see for himself. And I had Barbara dress up in her grandmother's clothes and walk back and forth on the cliffs."

Barbara buried her face in her hands with a moan. "All the time I was obeying you, I was torturing Russell Kincaid," she whispered. "He must have been terrified!"

"Didn't he deserve it?" John cried. "He murdered your grandmother! All I wanted was revenge!"

He paused for a moment, and no one said a word. When he spoke again, his voice was barely audible.

"The thing is, I never realized how far it would go. I thought he'd think he was losing his mind, that he'd back down and quit the race. It never occurred to me that he would try to push her over the cliffs again. I never dreamed he'd end up dead."

John Kincaid began to sob—loud, racking sobs.

Barbara couldn't stay quiet anymore. "That isn't true! You knew what you were doing to him—to all of us! But you didn't care! He may have swindled you out of money, but you took his *life!*"

John lifted his head and stared at her, and for the first time a look of remorse crossed his face. "You're right," he whispered. "I didn't care. I hated him for what he did to me. I wanted to destroy him, even if it meant destroying innocent lives—yours, your friends', Josine's."

The tape recorder came to a stop with a click, and silence descended. There was nothing more to be said. John Kincaid had confessed.

Fourteen

Friday morning all the Wakefields went to the hospital to bring Elizabeth home—all but Jessica, that is, who had been at the police station until two the night before.

Elizabeth, on crutches because of her ankle, rapped on the door of Jessica's bedroom. "I can't believe you can sleep at a time like this," she cried, limping into the room and sitting down on the edge of her twin's bed. "Wake up and tell me what I missed last night!"

Jessica groaned. "I'm sleeping," she protested, burying her head deeper in the pillow. But the next minute she remembered the events of the previous night and sat up straight, practically knocking Elizabeth off the bed. "You're home!

You're OK!" she cried joyfully, throwing her arms around her sister.

"Hey, watch out," Elizabeth said. "I have a concussion. Dr. Fisherman says I have to be very careful."

"But you're all right now, aren't you?" Jessica asked anxiously.

"Yes, I'm fine, Jess. I don't have a skull fracture or anything. But I want to hear all about what happened at the police station from you. I read in the newspaper that they caught John Kincaid."

"Yep," Jessica said, rubbing the sleep from her eyes. "And things look pretty bad for him. He's being held without bail, and they were reading off so many charges, I couldn't keep them straight. You should've heard him, Liz. He actually confessed to trying to drive his brother mad by making him believe Barbara was her grandmother."

"That's incredible!" Elizabeth cried. "Where's Barbara now?"

"She went back to Bayview House, believe it or not. Nicholas wanted her to go home with him, but she said she wanted to see Josine. She was really insistent." Jessica sighed. "They seem so in love, Liz. I guess they're going to get together today, since it's her birthday and everything."

"That's right," Elizabeth said. "I forgot about that, given all the excitement."

She unfolded the newspaper she had brought with her from the hospital and showed it to her sister. "Check this out," she said, pointing to the headline. "Russell Kincaid, Candidate for Mayor, Drowned!"

The story covered the entire front page of the local paper. "Possible suicide," read one story; another described John Kincaid's arrest under the subheading "Did Kincaid's Brother Cause His Death?"

But none of the stories described what had really happened. "I've already called Seth," Elizabeth told her twin. "I know we told Mom and Dad we wouldn't go to work today, Jess, but I told Seth if he came over here, we could give him the entire story from beginning to end."

Jessica nodded, her eyes shining. "Maybe they'll put our picture on the front page," she said hopefully.

Elizabeth gave her a look. "I doubt it, Jess. But at least we can help the *News* be the first paper to get the facts straight on Kincaid's death."

Jessica shivered. "Liz, every time I think about

what happened last night—I mean, you didn't see it. But the look on Kincaid's face when he was falling back from that cliff—" She bit her lip and hugged her knees close to her. "I had a really awful dream about it."

Elizabeth nodded, her eyes big. "Me, too. Dr. Fisherman said it's normal to have bad dreams after going through something like this." She sighed. "I think it's going to be a long, long time before I forget what happened at Bayview House."

"I wonder what's going to happen to Barbara now," Jessica said suddenly. "Is she going to spend the rest of the summer with Josine? I guess now that Kincaid is in jail, she's free to do what she wants."

Elizabeth nodded slowly, a thoughtful expression on her face. Jessica was right. It hadn't occurred to her until then, but there really wasn't any reason for Barbara to stay in Ronoma.

"She'll probably want to get away from Bayview House," Elizabeth mused. "As bad as it was for us, it was nothing compared to what Barbara went through. God, Jess, imagine almost being pulled off that cliff. I bet she can't wait to get away from that old house."

"Well, Nicholas won't be happy if she leaves."

"You're right, Jess. I guess we'll just have to wait and see what happens."

Barbara woke late on Friday morning. Sunlight was flooding through her bedroom window, and she could hear the sound of waves lapping gently against the rocks.

Only then did the horrible events of the previous night come flooding back to her. She sat up with a start, clapping her hand over her mouth, stifling a cry as she remembered Kincaid's grasp, pulling her back over the cliff. . . .

But it was all right, she told herself sternly. She was safe. Russell Kincaid was dead, his brother was in jail, and the horrible ordeal was over.

"Can I come in, Barbara?" Josine said softly, tapping at her door.

"Of course, Josine," Barbara said, swinging her legs over the side of the bed and scooping up Rory, who had spent the night curled beside her. She kissed her precious dog on the top of his head, then looked up at the old housekeeper with a smile.

"Oh, Josine," she cried when she saw that Josine had brought up a breakfast tray and a bunch of roses.

189

"The flowers are from that nice young man," Josine said, setting down the tray. "For your birthday. Did you forget it was today? He came this morning, left these, and said he'd be back in a few hours. He just wanted to make sure you were all right." Josine ducked her head shyly. "He cares for you so much," she added gently. "He reminds me—" She paused. "He's a little the way Jack used to be, before . . ."

"Before my grandmother died?" Barbara said gently.

Josine took a deep breath, pulling a wicker chair up so she could sit close to Barbara. "Yes," she murmured.

"Josine, does it hurt to talk about her? You don't have to if you don't want to." Barbara put her hand on Josine's arm. "It's just—well, I'd love to know more about her. I came here this summer hoping to learn more about my past. But it was all so horrible. John Kincaid made things such a nightmare for both of us, didn't he?"

"He did," Josine said softly. "He knew how easily I get confused, and he knew I was too weak to get in his way."

Barbara jumped out of bed and threw her arms around the old woman. "Oh, Josine. My heart breaks when I think of what he put you

190

through!" Her eyes filled with tears. "It was hard for me, but I've been here such a short time. For you . . . how long has he been threatening you?"

Josine shook her head. "Not so long. Before you came he gave me a terrible lecture. He promised nothing would happen to you as long as I went along with whatever he said. Sometimes"—she bit her lip—"he made me pretend to be senile so you wouldn't rely on me." She smiled sadly. "My memory isn't very good, but it's nowhere as bad as he made me pretend." She hugged Barbara to her. "Poor little thing. The minute I saw you I remembered every detail of that terrible summer."

"Josine, tell me about it. Tell me your version of what happened," Barbara begged her.

Josine looked sadly out the window at the cliffs. "It was such a waste," she whispered. "Your grandmother was a beautiful, vibrant young woman. She had her whole life in front of her. She fell madly in love with Jack, and he adored her. He wanted to marry her immediately, but Barbara insisted it would ruin his chances to work with her father. You see, Paul Lazarow was protective of his only child. She was afraid he wouldn't have kept Jack on as an apprentice if he knew they were in love."

191

"So they were married secretly?" Barbara asked.

Josine nodded. "Yes. And a few months later Barbara went away. She had a friend in Switzerland she said she was going to live with for a year. And Jack went with her. None of us knew they were together. They left because they'd found out she was going to have a baby. Their plan was to come back with the baby, hoping that her father would be won over then and would let Jack continue to study with him.

"But it all turned out so tragically," she continued sadly. "The baby girl was beautiful. Barbara named her Gwen."

"My mother," Barbara whispered.

Josine nodded. "Such a perfect little child. She and Jack adored that baby. You could just see how happy the three of them were. And how it sickened Russell Kincaid. He had wanted Barbara for himself. He said he loved her, but I never believed he really loved anyone but himself. And he swore if he couldn't have her, no one would."

"He and Jack were rivals, weren't they?" Barbara asked Josine.

The old housekeeper nodded "Yes. Jack was the more talented of the two. And Jack . . . well, he had a kind of sweet disposition that

192

made everyone love him. Everyone but Russell. Even then Russell was an unhappy, brooding young man. He set out to destroy this beautiful young family.

"None of us knew exactly how it happened," she went on. "Paul—Barbara's father—was already very sick, though he didn't know yet that he had cancer. He was upstairs in bed. I remember Jack had the baby. We were planning a surprise dinner for Barbara's birthday. And Russell called her outside, said he had something to tell her. That was the last thing we knew. Kincaid claimed she slipped on the wet rocks, that he'd tried to catch her, but it was no use. There were no witnesses."

"And Kincaid wasn't accused?" Barbara cried.

Josine shook her head. "He was suspected for a short time. There was an inquest. But, you see, two terrible things happened right after your grandmother's death. The first was that Paul, her father, found out he had liver cancer. He didn't live very long—maybe six months."

She sighed. "I used to think his will to live disappeared when Barbara died. In any case, he wasn't well enough to go through a lengthy trial. And because there were no witnesses, it would have been almost impossible to convict Kincaid. So Paul died believing Barbara's death had been an accident. And maybe in some ways that was best."

"What about Jack?" Barbara demanded.

Josine wiped her eyes. "That was the saddest thing of all," she said. "I can't describe to you what happened to Jack Pearsall. That night, the night of Barbara's birthday, I was the one who had to tell him she had drowned. He let out a cry unlike anything I'd ever heard before. Then he locked himself in the studio with the baby girl. He wouldn't let anyone near him. We were afraid—" She paused to wipe at her tears. "We were afraid the baby would die. We had to get the police to break into the studio. And, by then, Jack had gone out of his mind with grief."

Barbara stared at her. "You mean . . ."

"He couldn't say a word. He just sat there, completely dumb. Nothing seemed to bring him back. He was like that for months."

"So that's why my mother was raised by Du-Pres," Barbara whispered. "We never really knew or understood . . ."

"DuPres was the man that Barbara's girlfriend in Switzerland married. They had been named legal guardians of little Gwendolyn, and when it became apparent that Jack wasn't fit to take care of his own daughter, they took her with them to Europe." Josine looked searchingly at Barbara. "You never knew any of this?"

"None of it. My mother knew her mother had died in a tragic accident—and that was all she ever told me. She never mentioned Jack, her father. Josine, where is he now?"

Josine bit her lip. "He's in a rest home about an hour from here," she replied. "Barbara, he never fully recovered from the shock. Initially he was in a hospital. Paul left money in his will so that Jack, whom he'd forgiven completely, would always be taken care of. Jack stayed in the hospital for two years, then moved into this rest home. He never wanted to live in the outside world again. He's lived in the home for the past thirty-eight years. He's still painting. Some of the work he's done is extraordinary. But he was never the same man again. I've visited him once or twice a month for all these years. Sometimes"—she sighed—"he's all right, but sometimes he doesn't even know who I am."

"Do you think—Josine, could I see him?" Barbara cried.

Josine shook her head and studied Barbara sadly. "But why?" she asked gently. "Darling, I'm not sure he'd be able to talk to you. He's weak, his mind isn't really—"

"But I want to see him," Barbara insisted.

"Please, Josine. Tell me where the rest home is."

Barbara knew then and there she had to see Jack Pearsall. She couldn't explain why to Josine, but she knew she wouldn't rest until she had laid eyes on him.

She had come to Ronoma for the summer to learn about her past. And though she had almost gotten trapped in a nightmare, she had discovered her history after all. Now she wanted to touch part of that history.

And her grandfather was all of that world that was left.

Fifteen

"Barbara!" Nicholas cried, running across the lawn in front of Bayview House to wrap her in his arms.

It was late Friday morning, and Nicholas had been out in Ronoma for hours. The first time he had come to the house, Josine had told him that Barbara was still asleep. After leaving the roses for her, he went into Denning to take a walk and try to clear his mind.

"Happy birthday," he said, kissing her tenderly. "Whoever could have guessed last night that we'd be out here today in the sunlight, hugging each other? That I'd be wishing you happy birthday like nothing out of the ordinary had ever happened?"

Barbara clutched him tightly. "Don't let go of

me," she whispered fiercely. Rory leaped around them, barking excitedly.

"Listen to me," Nicholas said, leading her over to the steps in front of the house and sitting down with her there. "We have some very serious planning to do. Because"—he searched her face—"if you're feeling OK—if you're not too worn out or frightened from last night—I want to help you celebrate your birthday in the most wonderful way imaginable."

Barbara pressed his hand and smiled. "Just being with you is enough," she said. "But, Nicholas, there *is* something I want to do today."

"Anything you want!" Nicholas cried without hesitating.

Suddenly shy, Barbara fiddled with her bracelet. "I had a long talk with Josine this morning. It turns out that most of the time she was pretending to be senile. John Kincaid threatened her, made her act confused so I wouldn't rely on her for information." She shook her head. "What a villain that man is!"

"Well, now he's in jail," Nicholas declared vehemently. "You don't have to worry about him anymore."

Barbara nodded. "Anyway, Josine told me that Jack—Barbara's husband—my grandfather —is in a rest home not too far from here. He

198

never recovered after my grandmother's death."
Her eyes were full of sympathy and sorrow.
"That's why his daughter, my mother, was taken
to Switzerland and raised by her legal guardians. Nicholas, I want to see him. Today, on my
birthday. I want to hug my grandfather."

Nicholas looked uneasy for a moment. "Are
you sure it's all right? It wouldn't upset him, or
you, too much?"

Barbara shook her head. "Josine goes to see
him fairly often. She says he's OK. Weak, but
OK. He still paints. He's sold a number of paintings. But he never wanted to leave the rest
home." She paused, then looked deeply into
Nicholas's eyes. "I really need to see him," she
said. "Nicholas, will you come with me? I've
gotten directions to the home, and I called ahead.
His nurse said she would talk to him for a
while, prepare him for my visit." She cleared
her throat. "I want you to come with me."

Nicholas clutched her hand. "You know I'll
do whatever you want," he said warmly. "Of
course I'll go with you."

Barbara was silent for a minute. She looked
away, then blurted out, "My parents called this
morning to wish me a happy birthday." She
gulped. "I told them a little bit about what

happened. Not everything, because I knew how frightened they'd be."

Nicholas nodded, still holding her hand.

"They want me to come home," Barbara whispered, staring at the ground. "They're cutting their own trip short."

"Home?" Nicholas repeated blankly. At first he didn't think he'd heard her right.

"They're calling travel agents already, arranging the whole thing," Barbara said, her eyes filling with tears. "I didn't want to say anything until later, Nicholas, but I can't keep anything from you." She brushed the tears from her eyes. "Daddy's calling the home where my grandfather is. They want him to come back to Switzerland with me. My mother wants him to live with us."

"Switzerland," Nicholas repeated dumbly. He clutched her hand. "Can't you wait just a few weeks, Barbara? Think how wonderful it would be to spend time together now that Kincaid is gone. We could meet anywhere, go anywhere, I could show you my home—"

"Please, Nicholas, don't," Barbara whispered. "Don't think about things that can never take place." She reached her hand up to touch his face. "I don't know why this has happened to us. Why couldn't it have been simple from the start?"

"Barbara, I love you," Nicholas cried, pulling her into his arms and holding her.

Suddenly his earlier mood of euphoria struck him as incredibly foolish. How could he have been so elated, believing they had finally escaped everything that had been in their way?

It had honestly never occurred to Nicholas that she would leave him so soon, that after fighting and fighting to save her, she would just vanish, as if she really had been a ghost after all, leaving nothing behind but memories.

"Oh, don't look so sad, Nicholas, please," Barbara begged him. "Let's make our time together as happy as possible." They walked hand in hand down to the road where his Jeep was parked.

And let's make it last as long as possible, Nicholas thought, squeezing her hand tightly.

The rest home where Jack Pearsall had been living for the past thirty-eight years was an hour's drive south. The California scenery was beautiful: mountains in the distance, an occasional view of the Pacific, lush foliage, and farmland dotted with palm trees.

The home itself looked more like a country inn than anything else. It was nestled discreetly away from the road in a wooded glade.

"You must be Barbara," the nurse at the entrance desk greeted her.

Barbara nodded. "And this is my friend Nicholas." Her eyes were grave. "How is my grandfather taking all this? Is he shocked that I'm here?"

The nurse seemed to choose her words carefully. "Actually, we were all anxious to see how he'd react. You know, he's lived here without any excitement for so many years. Josine comes to see him now and then, but that's all. He paints. He takes walks. He has conversations with some of the others who live here. He isn't really ill anymore, but he's fragile." She patted Barbara on the arm. "He's overjoyed that your mother is alive and well and has a family of her own. And he can't wait to see you. There's just one thing."

"What's that?" Barbara asked anxiously. "I don't want to do anything to upset him!"

The nurse studied Barbara with concern. "You must know how much you look like her—like his wife. Of course, I never saw her. But I've seen photographs. And Jack has a painting of her in his room. I'm afraid he may be startled by the resemblance when he first sees you, that's all."

Barbara nodded. She squeezed Nicholas's hand to show him she wasn't afraid.

"If you think it's all right," she said softly, "I want to try. I don't know why I feel so sure of this, but I think it'll be all right."

The nurse smiled. "Fine. Let me take you both to his room."

Barbara and Nicholas followed her down a long sunlit corridor. At the end she stopped and knocked gently on the door. "Jack? Your granddaughter and her friend are here to see you," she said.

Silence greeted this announcement.

"I'll leave you with him," the nurse whispered. "Just go on in. I'll be right down the hall if you need me."

Nicholas stepped back so Barbara could go in first. She pushed the door open, took a deep breath, and tiptoed into the room.

"Grandfather?" she said in a small, nervous voice.

Jack Pearsall was standing with his back to them, looking out the window at the garden. His room was large and spacious, with a small bed off to one side. He obviously used most of the room as a studio. Paintings lined the walls, and one, half-finished, was set up on an easel.

The painting Nicholas couldn't take his eyes off was hanging over a small desk. It was Barbara, down to the last detail! But unlike the painting by Lazarow that he had seen at the museum, this portrait was filled with joy. Barbara's head was flung back, and she was laughing.

Finally Jack turned around. He was a remarkably handsome man, his hair mostly gray, his face lined, but his eyes a lovely shade of blue. He stared at Barbara without speaking, and Nicholas felt her hand tremble in his.

She swallowed hard and took one timid step closer.

Jack cleared his throat with an effort. Then his eyes flooded with tears, and he crossed the room in two strides and engulfed his granddaughter in his arms.

"I'm sorry," he murmured, wiping his eyes. "They said you looked like her, but I had no idea . . ."

Nicholas stared at the painting over the desk, and a lump formed in his throat. For the first time in his life, he thought that he had some inkling of what it meant to love someone with that kind of passion. Jack Pearsall had loved Barbara all his life. He had stayed out here in this lonesome place, cut off from the rest of the world, reliving forty-year-old memories. It was as if he had died when Barbara died.

"I painted that the month before she died," Jack said softly, turning to look at Nicholas.

"It's beautiful," Nicholas said. "You've captured such beauty and life in the painting."

Jack cleared his throat. "Thank you. I've lived here alone for so long, forgive me, I'm not much good at talking. Not with young people." He paused. "I was ruined when she died," he whispered. "I was too weak. I used to tell her that she was the one with the strength, and she'd laugh, just as she's laughing there, in that picture." He put his arm around Barbara. "You see, she was the strongest, bravest, funniest girl who ever lived. Nothing scared her. Not even Russell Kincaid. She thought he was a fool." He shook his head. "If she could see me now, if she only knew . . ."

Jack took a deep breath. "I saw the news today. I know he's dead."

Barbara nodded. She found it too difficult to speak.

Jack shook his head. "I was shocked when I heard it. I used to think I wanted revenge. I used to fantasize that I was strong enough to find Kincaid and kill him." He sighed. "And you know what? When I heard he was dead last night, I got tears in my eyes. Because he suffered, in the end. He was a man full of hate and bitterness, and he suffered."

"Oh, Grandpa," Barbara cried, throwing her arms around him. "I told my mother about finding you," she whispered, staring up at him. "She wants you to come back with me to Switzerland. She wants you to live with us."

Jack stared down at her. "Gwen?" he said softly, his eyes wide.

Barbara nodded. "Will you come, Grandpa? We all want you to."

Jack stared helplessly from her to Nicholas and back to her again. "All these years I've lived in the past," he whispered. "I didn't realize what a curse I'd put on myself, not letting go. I wouldn't live in the world because the world had destroyed the woman I loved. Now" —he looked at Barbara with bewilderment— "this beautiful granddaughter teaches me that it isn't too late—that I can hold my daughter in my arms again before I die."

The next minute Barbara and her grandfather were hugging each other and crying and laughing at the same time.

Jack turned back to look at the painting. "You

know," he said, clearing his throat, "today was her birthday."

Barbara and Nicholas exchanged glances.

"We know," they said, smiling at each other.

Looking at Barbara and Jack, Nicholas thought that perhaps it was possible to live in the present without losing the past at all.

Then he remembered that Barbara was leaving, and the lump rose again in his throat.

It seemed to Nicholas that once they left the rest home, things happened with amazing speed. Phone calls to Switzerland confirmed that Jack would indeed be returning with Barbara. Tickets and flights were arranged, and by early evening it was all set: Barbara and her grandfather would be flying back to Geneva on Sunday. Josine would stay in Bayview House for the time being. Jack eventually wanted to turn the house into a museum for Paul Lazarow's paintings.

"Sunday," Nicholas murmured, staring at Barbara with disbelief.

Barbara shook her head. "I can't believe it either," she said softly. "My parents are so frightened and confused by everything that's happened. They're very anxious to see me, and my grandfather. They're flying back to Geneva today."

Nicholas swallowed the lump in his throat. "Two days," he said dully. "Do you realize in two days you'll be on the plane, and I'll be here alone without you?"

Barbara didn't respond. "Let's take a walk," she suggested.

Nicholas fingered the tissue-paper package in his pocket. It was a gift for Barbara—something he had chosen for her earlier in the week. He hadn't found the right moment to give it to her yet.

"OK," he said.

They walked companionably through the woods, out to the cliffs behind the house. "I can't believe this is the same place where Kincaid died last night," Barbara said. The water looked so calm now, and the sunlight bounced off the cliffs, making everything sparkle. "Can you, Nicholas? Isn't it amazing how things have turned out?"

Nicholas bit his lip. "Barbara, doesn't it break your heart to think we're going to be separated?"

Barbara looked out over the cliff. "It does," she said finally. "It makes me so sad that if I think about it too hard, I won't be able to go on. But, Nicholas, remember what Jack said.

208

We can't live in the past. We have our whole lives in front of us." She gazed out at the dazzling water. "If I've learned anything these past few weeks, it's that life is incredibly precious. Nobody knows what's going to happen from day to day." She grasped his hand. "We'll see each other again, Nicholas. I know we will. I'll be coming back with Jack and my parents to set up the museum at Bayview House. And no matter what, you and I will always be friends!"

Nicholas removed the package from his pocket and handed it to her.

"What's this?" she cried.

"It's for your birthday," Nicholas murmured. He watched as she tore off the pink tissue paper, then opened a small white box.

"It's beautiful!" she exclaimed.

It was a small gold locket on a chain, very simple, with two sets of initials intertwined together on the face—Barbara's and his own. Barbara traced the initials with her finger. Neither of them spoke.

At last Nicholas tipped her face up to his and looked deeply into her eyes. "Promise you'll always remember this moment," he said tenderly.

"I could never forget," she said, her eyes filling with tears.

Then he took her in his arms. "What Jack

said about living in the past is true. But something else is true, too." He ran his fingers through her hair. "Love—the kind of love we feel—doesn't happen very often. Sometimes it only happens once. I don't want to live in the past, and I don't want you to, either. But I don't want to forget the power of what I'm feeling right now."

"Oh, Nicholas," Barbara cried.

Their lips met in a deep and gentle kiss. Nicholas could feel her heart pounding against his. It was like the rhythm of the waves—steady, strong, unforgettable, a kind of music that would be with him for the rest of his life.

Sixteen

"It feels strange to be back at work," Elizabeth mused on Monday morning. She looked at the crutches leaning up against her desk and shook her head. "If it weren't for my ankle, and the fact that my head still hurts a little, I think I'd have a hard time believing that any of that stuff at Bayview House really happened."

Jessica nodded. "I know what you mean." She thumbed through the pile of notes on her desk. "But now that I've got to put all of this into some kind of order for Dan, I think I'm going to be reliving most of what happened."

Elizabeth laughed. She could sympathize with her twin on that point. Mr. Robb had called a meeting for that afternoon to discuss the Kincaid story, and the twins were expected to assemble all their notes and be prepared to make presentations to the editors.

"Did you talk to Nicholas yet today?" Jessica asked.

"No." Elizabeth frowned. "Not since last night just after Barbara's plane left. He didn't sound too good, frankly. I made him promise he'd come by the office today so we could take him out for lunch."

Jessica chewed on the end of her pen. "Poor Nicholas. I don't think I've ever seen anyone so much in love."

Elizabeth was about to comment when Seth came over, a big smile on his face.

"How does it feel to be part of a heroic twinship?" he teased, throwing down that day's copy of the paper.

"Look! Our pictures are in there!" Jessica squealed, snatching the paper.

"Let me see," Elizabeth cried, looking over her shoulder. Sure enough, there was a slightly grainy photo of Elizabeth, Jessica, and Nicholas. The headline below it read, "Local Teens Crack Revenge Story!" And the accompanying story described the events leading up to Kincaid's death.

"Where was that picture taken? I look weird," Jessica cried, scanning the article eagerly.

"I think it was at the company picnic," Elizabeth murmured.

"Hey, Seth," Jessica said, "I don't want to be picky or anything, but why does Elizabeth come before Jessica here?"

Elizabeth and Seth cracked up. "Ever heard of alphabetical order?" Elizabeth asked her sister.

Seth perched himself on the edge of Elizabeth's desk. "Listen, I just came from Mr. Robb's office. It looks like our work for the next few weeks is going to be different than we'd planned. After all, now that Kincaid is dead, Robinson will be running uncontested. So there isn't much coverage to do on the campaign anymore. And the research is finished on Lazarow."

Elizabeth listened expectantly.

"That means we're going to have to think about reassigning you two," Seth continued. "In the meantime, Mr. Robb wants you two to write a collaborative story on your experience with Kincaid and his brother. Do you think you can do that?"

"Collaborate? How can we possibly do that?"

Elizabeth giggled. "You mean you don't think you can work with me, Jess?"

"Well, I guess I can."

Seth looked sober for a minute. "We heard from police headquarters this morning. John Kincaid's trial date has been moved up. You two can keep your eyes on that as it approaches, too." He turned to leave but seemed to remember one last thing. "Oh, yeah. What about Barbara and her grandfather? Do you think you could interview them for your story?"

"I'm afraid not, Seth," Elizabeth said sadly, looking at her twin. "Barbara left for Geneva last night. And her grandfather—Jack Pearsall—flew back with her."

Elizabeth and Jessica met Nicholas in the lobby of the Western Building at noon. Elizabeth was pleased to see he looked subdued but composed, and he smiled when he saw them approaching.

They entered the coffee shop, and Nicholas helped Elizabeth lean her crutches against the table as she sat down. "How much longer do you need to be on those things?" he asked her.

"The doctor said another week. I did a pretty good job on the sprain," Elizabeth answered with a wry smile.

Once they were all seated, Jessica didn't waste any time. "Nicholas, are you all right? Was it terrible saying goodbye?"

Nicholas laughed. "That's what I love about you, Jess. No beating around the bush."

Elizabeth gave her twin a reproving glance. "Maybe Nicholas doesn't want to talk about it right now, Jess," she said.

But Nicholas brushed this off. "No, Liz, it's fine. Actually, I'm glad to be able to talk about it with you guys—because you knew her. My parents don't really understand how I feel."

"It must've been incredibly hard for you both," Elizabeth said gently.

Nicholas nodded. "It was. Actually, it was one of the hardest things I've ever done. At the airport I went with her as far as they'd let me. Her grandfather stood away from us while we said goodbye. But neither of us could bear to part. We just hung on to each other. Finally we heard over the loudspeaker that everyone on that flight to Geneva had to board, and she slipped out of my arms." Nicholas bit his lip. Then, with real effort, he continued. "That was when Jack Pearsall saved the day. He told me he had a present for me that he had put in the back of my Jeep. 'Go look,' he said. 'Maybe it'll make some of this easier!'"

"What was it?" the twins asked in unison.

"Well, it's still there, in the back of my Jeep. I wanted you two to see it. Liz, are you good enough on those crutches to come outside and take a look?"

"Absolutely," Elizabeth cried.

A few minutes later the twins watched Nicholas open the back of his Jeep and gingerly withdraw something large, wrapped in a blanket. They moved closer to see what it was, and Elizabeth gasped.

"It's a portrait of Barbara!"

Jack had given Nicholas the beautiful portrait of Barbara that had been hanging over his desk.

"There was a note with it, too," Nicholas said, handing it to the twins.

" 'Dear Nicholas,' " Elizabeth read aloud. " 'I want you to have this. Not as a memorial, as it was for me, but as a reminder that the past is always alive in the present. Live for the present, Nicholas. If love has a lesson for us, that's what it is.' "

"That's beautiful," Elizabeth murmured.

Jessica nodded in agreement. "What a wonderful portrait," she said.

Nicholas stood back, admiring the painting. His voice was full of emotion when he finally spoke. "Jack is right," he said. "Living in the present is what's most important. But I'll tell you one thing, you two. I'm never going to forget Barbara. Not as long as I live."

Elizabeth pressed her sister's hand. She knew that she wouldn't either. Not Barbara, not Bayview House, not any of the events they had been through together since that fateful day they first brought Nicholas out to Ronoma.

YOUR OWN

SLAM BOOK!

If you've read *Slambook Fever*, Sweet Valley High #48, you know that slam books are the rage at Sweet Valley High. Now *you* can have a slam book of your own! Make up your own categories, such as "Biggest Jock" or "Best Looking," and have your friends fill in the rest! There's a four-page calendar, horoscopes and questions most asked by Sweet Valley readers with answers from Elizabeth and Jessica

It's a must for SWEET VALLEY fans!

☐ 05496 **FRANCINE PASCAL'S SWEET VALLEY HIGH SLAM BOOK**
Laurie Pascal Wenk   **$3.50**
